Between Life and Death
The In-Betweener

Book One

Ann Christy

Originally published as The In-Betweener
Copyright © 2015, 2016 by Ann Christy

ISBN-13: 978-1539678151
ISBN-10: 1539678156

www.AnnChristy.com

Also by Ann Christy

For Gabe
You are the one I would
want on my side
during the zombie apocalypse.
Totally.

One Month Ago - Recon

"Did you find food?" Veronica asks, her hands clutching at her belly.

It's either an unconscious expression of hunger or simple anxiety, but Sam would bet it's hunger. It's been two days since any of them had a full belly.

Jon, his solemn, two-year-old face drawn and pinched, tucks himself into the girl's side. As always, he is quiet—far too quiet for a child his age—but Sam can read the hunger etched there even without words.

Sam hands her the sack he's holding. It's woefully light, but he smiles anyway and says, "Enough for a few days."

His smile is wide and bright, the smile of someone who doesn't want anyone around him to be sad, but his eyes carry hints of the worry he keeps stuffed inside. Five faces watch him carefully, five young faces he loves.

Ranging in age from two-year-old Jon to the almost-grown Veronica, they watch without judgment, only hope. Sam wants nothing more than to have come home with too much food to carry, but it's just not there to find anymore. He schools his expression in a way he hopes will appear as if there is food aplenty, just waiting to be found. They can't know how bad it still is outside these safe walls. He won't allow hope to be taken from them too.

It's almost all they have left.

Veronica opens the sack with eager hands and then gasps at the contents. Rice fills the bottom and packets of dry soup mix poke out of the top of the grains. "Can I cook it?" she asks, a little too eagerly.

"Of course! Let's chow," Sam answers, ruffling her hair.

Jeremy, the studious one, folds his book to his chest like a small professor disturbed during non-office hours. He clears his throat to get Sam's attention.

Sam picks up Piper and she throws her arms around his neck. The simple pleasure she takes in giving and receiving affection is one of the only truly uncomplicated things in their lives.

"Yeah, Jeremy," Sam says, and tickles Piper under her chin. Her eyes carry the typical cant of a Down Syndrome child, and her words are sometimes a little blurry, but she's always the bright light in his day and she's managing things surprisingly well.

"Uh, did you see her?" Jeremy asks.

Shooting a glance Jeremy's way to let him know that the time to talk about that would come later, he relents at the disappointed look on the boy's face and gives him a single, tiny nod. That seems to be enough for Jeremy, because he grins and settles back down by the sliding glass door. The light streams through the thin sheet hung there and he can see to read. He has his books and favorite blankets there, almost like a nest that proclaims the area is his territory.

Penny, three years old and his little angel, bangs her blocks together and then knocks over the tower that she and Veronica had been building in the center of the main room. She laughs a high, pealing laugh and Sam puts Piper down to rush over to the spot where Penny is playing.

"*Shh*, baby girl. Remember the quiet rules?"

She hands him a blue block and puts her finger to her lips, her little-girl smile breaking out behind the stubby, dirty finger.

After the children are settled once more, the excitement of his return now passed, Sam goes to the kitchen to explain to Veronica what she must have already seen for herself. She's bent over a cookie sheet and picking debris out of the grains of rice.

She looks up at his entrance and says, "That bad, huh?"

At fifteen, Veronica is nearly an adult. After two years during which she lost her family, found a new family in Sam and the other children, and become adept at hiding in silence, she is not easily fooled. He nods. She sighs, shakes her head, and bends back to her task.

"Grab another cookie sheet and help if you want."

Sam grins at her bowed head. Coming from anyone else, those words might sound like there was some option involved in the statement. When said by Veronica, he understands it for what it is.

If you've got time to stand there, you've got time to sort rice.

Jeremy's shadow falls between their bowed heads and the cookie sheets a few minutes later. It's no mystery to Sam what's on Jeremy's mind. The kid wants to talk about the strange girl at the warehouse. A girl who might be dangerous or who might be their salvation.

Jeremy, though only twelve, was on his own outside for far longer than Veronica. He's at least as experienced in this new world as the teenager, if not more. But he *is* only twelve and it's hard for Sam to decide how much he should share. How much uncertainty? How much fear? How much hope?

It seems to Sam he's always walking a fine line when discussing their situation. Sure, Veronica and Jeremy are old enough to have a voice in decisions. But he also wants to spare them whatever he can of the horrors waiting just outside their door. Most of the time, he winds up sharing more than he feels he should.

The truth—if Sam is honest with himself—is that he feels even less prepared for this world than he supposes these two kids must be. At twenty-four, he had lived in his first apartment alone (this apartment). He'd just finished his first year at his first job (teaching at Piper's school). His biggest worry had been how to manage his laundry (once his mom stopped doing it for him). Now, he has five kids in a world in which there is nothing except deadheads and the as-yet-not-quite-dead afflicted. And the six of them. And now, the girl at the warehouse.

"So, you saw her?" Jeremy asks without preamble.

Picking out something that looks suspiciously like a mouse turd from the rice, Sam flicks it into the waste bucket between him and Veronica. Without looking up, he says, "I did. She's still there. I'm pretty sure she's living there alone."

"Hmm," Jeremy *hmms*. He isn't satisfied. That little *hmm* says it all.

Putting aside the tray, Sam sighs and says, "Okay. I'm pretty sure she lives alone and I'm pretty sure that warehouse has food in it because she looks good."

Veronica gives him a sidelong glance, the barest hint of a sly smile on her face. "Good, huh?"

"Gah, you're disgusting. I mean she looks well fed."

"Do you think it's safe to talk to her?" Jeremy asks. The crease between his eyes is so constant that he's getting a permanent line there. He's had more bad experiences with people—the living kind—since the world went to crap than the rest of them put together. He's desperate for safety, yet desperately afraid of meeting new people. And meeting more people is the only path to the safety Jeremy craves—which sort of puts them all in a bind.

Sam considers the question. *Do we stay quiet and keep to ourselves while we starve, or make contact with new people who might turn on us and kill us? What a choice.*

During this last trip, he'd watched her for a full day and stayed close enough to observe the general area all night. He wanted to get all the information he could on this trip, because he intended it to be the last one. The next time he came to the warehouses where the girl lived, he would be bringing the kids with him. So, it was worth the long time away from the kids to watch her and be sure about her. With binoculars his only tool, and settled in the dubious comfort of a tree, he'd worried about the kids through the night. What he saw had confused him. He'd watched her plenty of times before and thought he had her figured out. But when evening came, she did something that threw him for a loop. Now, he wasn't so sure about her.

She'd gone about her day in the exact same way she'd gone about her days when he watched her before. Her routine was consistent, which actually wasn't a good thing. Developing habits wasn't wise. If he could predict her routine, then people with less benign motives that came upon her could do the same.

Habits aside, the girl was an enigma to him. The way she did things was so clinical, as if it were nothing more than another day doing a job, like accounting or some other profession that didn't involve smashing up the unquiet dead. Every morning, rain or shine, she walked her perimeter and poked the heck out of the deadheads on her fence, looping wire over their necks and gesticulating extravagantly as she spoke to them.

Sometimes she whistled a tune while she did it.

Then, without fail, she went outside the fence and bashed all the deadheads in the brains over and over until they had no heads at all. And she whistled then too. Or sang. Or talked to the birds.

But yesterday, well, that had been a little different. In the evening, before the sun had fully set, at the exact moment the sky shifted to an amazing pink and orange blaze, she had dragged out a blanket-wrapped figure. She'd been crying—he could see that much through his binoculars—her oddly off-kilter eye red, swollen, and wandering, the scar on her head a vivid white under her black ponytail. She'd cried the whole way outside the fence to the place where she dumped the bodies of all the deadheads.

Then she'd unwrapped the blanket and Sam had trained his glasses on the body, thinking it might be another person, but it had been a deadhead more shriveled than any he'd seen. It looked like a human raisin. The head was smashed to a pulp, so that was no help in figuring out anything more about the deadhead, but the girl had hugged the deadhead. Really hugged it. She'd wept and straightened its clothes and talked to it, though Sam couldn't hear her words from his spot in the trees.

But despite all the emotional outpouring, in the end, as the light faded, she'd left it there and gone back inside her fence to her warehouse.

After that strange sight, Sam hadn't felt as sure about her. Up to that point, she'd seemed weird, but anyone who'd survived to this point had become a little odd. It was understandable. He was weird in his way too. They all were. But, after that scene of hers, with her mummy-like deader and her tears, what did he think of her now? Those were more the actions of someone gone well past odd and directly into crazy territory.

So, Sam doesn't know how he should answer Jeremy's question at all. Is it safe to approach her? Do they have the leisure any longer to worry whether it is or isn't entirely safe?

Sam looks at the mouse droppings and grit mixed in with the small bit of rice he was able to gather from the bottom of a long-since-looted cabinet.

No, their options are dwindling with each day that passes. So, he decides to go with the truth.

"I have no idea if it's safe or not. But at this point, I don't think we have a choice. This area is picked clean and we've got to get someplace where we can eat," Sam says.

"And grow food," Veronica adds.

"Yeah, and that too."

"So, we go?" Jeremy asks, his fingers working at the book, displaying his nervousness in spite of his calm voice.

"Soon," Sam says, and goes back to picking mouse turds out of their rice.

Today - Emily

The report of a gun is one of my favorite sounds. It's so powerful, so dangerous, yet perversely, it's also the sound of safety. I figured that in the unlikely event the world really *did* end, I'd at least have that. I could shoot all day long, make all the biggest, blasting shotgun sounds I wanted.

It turns out that I don't even get that. Before this freaking mess, I never feared firing a gun. It was a hobby, something my mother thought I might enjoy, something where I had all the control. Now? No way. The noise draws them like bees to a fresh patch of clover on a spring morning. Hearing is almost the last thing that goes, those little mechanical vibrations of tiny bones in the ears lasting longer than eyes that go gooey or dry out into little raisins.

Once the last sense goes, they mostly just stand around until they feel the vibration of something passing close by. Some wander, reaching out to touch things as they pass, tasting everything they touch. Without their senses, they have a hard time finding metal, not to mention animals. Animals, including humans, offer the best source of the nutrients they need. Most deaders are easy to get past now. Just walk quietly and don't roll a heavy wagon or anything.

I used to see overturned wagons from time to time, back when we still left the complex. I would have liked to tell people, but really, people are more dangerous than the deaders. And my mom wouldn't even entertain the notion of contacting other survivors. I painted warnings on a couple of signs, but that's as far as she'd let me go.

Nowadays, hidden as I am out here, I don't see people anymore and haven't in months. But if I did, I wouldn't tell them. I want to remain hidden because I'm alone and that has changed my views on the doing of neighborly deeds.

These days, I love silent weapons. Bows—particularly crossbows that I can actually draw—regular bows, big knives…you name it. I even had a bunch of those pistol crossbows for a while, but I ran out of bolts for them and left them behind when we abandoned the old law offices where we stayed for a long while. I liked the law offices. First off, no one loots a law office, and second, the couches and chairs were awesome for sleeping in.

My current favorites in the weapons department are handles—broom handles, rake handles, anything like that—with knives strapped to them using hose clamps. Lots of hose clamps. The big ones. I call these contraptions my bayonets.

It's my version of World War I redux. Total trench warfare, only without trenches.

I like silencers quite a lot too, but they aren't perfect. The sound they make isn't a sweet little *thut* like in the movies, just a more muffled sort of roar. But finding what I need to make them is getting harder and harder. Plastic bottles outside the complex crumble in my hands after two years in the elements and most steel wool was cleaned out of stores a long time ago by people who must have had the same idea I did.

In my warehouse, there is exactly zero steel wool, but bottles I've got plenty of. And I'm no longer tempted by substitutions. They rarely work like the movies suggested they would. Forget using potatoes. What a mess that is! And anyway, if I had potatoes now, I'd eat them. And pillows? Yeah, they catch fire, which is super inconvenient. And I don't even want to talk about what happened when I used the cotton batting left over in the sachet factory across from my home warehouse. Think floral-scented flames, burning in pretty colors that just seem *wrong* for fire, and you'll start to get the idea.

Before we got here—the land of candy bars and plastic-bottled energy drinks—I scrounged for anything I could use to shoot more quietly at greater range than I could with a bow. I'm a shooter and my bow skills are ones I've picked up since all this happened. Without my mom and a training manual we found at the place where we got our first bows, I wouldn't have any bow skills at all. It's strange to think this, but when we were first trying to learn how to use them, we had fun. Not having an arrow go up or to the side or simply fall down was a reason for high-fives and smiles. But quietly.

Crossbows are much easier. I like those. I still don't like shooting things that look like people, though.

The worst part is that they aren't all deaders. Deaders are a little easier to deal with. They look dead. They are clearly not there anymore, not thinking or really human. It's the in-betweeners that bother the crap out of me.

Maybe they're brain-dead and truly not themselves—not human—anymore, but their eyes are bright and moving, still blue or brown or green, and they focus when they see something. They still move with something like human grace, still seek something like shelter when they are cold or shade when they are hot. They avoid danger and run when I start firing arrows or bolts in their direction. And they scream when they get hit.

Sometimes, the in-betweeners make me cry.

Enough of that. Enough thinking. I can't go down that well. That's the way I think of it. When I start dwelling on things, it feels like I'm going down a well and the circle of light at the top gets smaller and smaller until it's like I won't be able to climb back out. I know it's really depression and if there's a shrink left in this world, I'm pretty sure that shrink would tell me I have every reason to be depressed.

Alas, depression does not help with survival, so I don't have time for it.

I need to make a supply run to the other buildings and do my daily rounds, so I shrug on my best scavenged backpack and grab another one to fit over my front. I can't work a bow—or a crossbow or anything else—with a full backpack hanging off my chest, so I put that one on last, with the straps on top, so that I can drop it quickly should the need arise. I don't expect trouble, but I'm always ready for it should it arrive. My head is full of aches and fog this morning, so I pop a couple of my dwindling supply of ibuprofen before going out into the light.

Through the window, the day is blossoming brightly. I lose sight of the sky while I make my way out of the office up on the observation deck inside the warehouse I call home. The light dims at the bottom of the stairs, so I walk carefully across the dark expanse to the door. That door is the only one I can use with relative safety because it's the only one with a window. A small square of glass set at just the right height to look out of, it's embedded with wire and quite thick. I love a good wire-mesh window.

Once the light leaking in from that small window is sufficient for me to see by, I walk with more care, trying to keep my footfalls light. That's surprisingly easy for me. Part of that is practice and part is due to my gear. The boots I'm wearing were once a part of my mother's military uniform. She broke them in until they reached a point of perfect comfort and now, they serve me well in my turn.

She once told me that her boots were an excellent metaphor for life in general. At the time, I was pretty sure she meant to make me feel better about the awkwardness of growing up and my appearance. Then, I'd been growing boobs and I got frequent leg-aches from rapid growth. Plus all the other stuff that goes with growing up.

I think she was trying to tell me that she thought I was beautiful, and that the awkwardness would pass.

What she said was that when her boots were new, they looked perfect with her uniform but were painful to wear, pinching her toes when she put them on and bringing up blisters when she walked in them. By the time those new boots got old and needed replacing, they looked terrible. They caused senior officers to give her the occasional pointed look, but they were as comfortable as bare feet. While the rest of her might ache at the end of a long day, her feet felt just fine.

In between those two states, her boots reached a point of perfection. She said that life was exactly the same. The beginning was hard to get through even though it looked like it should be smooth sailing. By the end, the person had long experience and had weathered the storms, but the appearance of things made it clear it was coming to an end. It's the long, glorious middle part, she said, that makes life worth living.

She's been dead for over a year now, but I only figured out what she was trying to say when I started wearing her boots. The awkwardness is gone and I'm definitely not pretty, but I've grown comfortable in my skills and in my skin. I'm positive she didn't mean this would happen before I turned nineteen—she was probably talking about middle age—but still, I understand it now. We grow into ourselves and eventually, if we just have some patience, we can feel comfortable as we are before we fade.

It's a nice thought and I hope—sometimes anyway—that I'll reach middle age and share that bit of wisdom with someone else. For now, things need doing and the area beyond the window is clear. So, no more mom-style philosophical meanderings. The workday's starting bell is ringing my tune.

Yesterday - The Walking Man

Why is it so hard to concentrate? Why does walking feel so awkward? Why does my body hurt so bad?

The man tries to keep to the center of the street, where there is more room for his unsteady progress and not as much litter to bedevil him. Tripping over everything no longer seems like something he can stop himself from doing. And the road looks so strange to his eyes. He knows there is something wrong, but exactly what that might be is beyond him at the moment. The colors are off, either washed out or too vivid by turns.

The sudden beat of nearby wings draws his attention. The urge inside him is immediate and utterly out of his control. He stumbles after the shapes, his hands squeezing as if he already has one in hand, but they're gone before he comes anywhere near them. The dark shapes flit against the too-bright sky and he can't seem to look away until the shapes finally disappear into the trees.

The car in front of him seems to rise up out of nowhere. He bangs into the side mirror hard enough to hear the splintering of plastic followed a microsecond later by the sickening, dull crack of his hip bone. When he looks down, he sees the car is dusty, its tires flat, and the gaps along the bottom choked with rotted leaves. It had been here the whole time.

Am I really so out of it that I didn't see a car? I must be sick.

The pain in his hip grows sharp and his hand seeks the spot. Blood seeps through his jeans but then stops quickly. At least it seems to, but the light looks different, as if time has passed while he's been standing there, one hand to his hip and his eyes following the leaves fluttering all over the street.

He fumbles with his shirt, trying to see the spot, but his hands won't cooperate. His fingers feel like sausages connected to his hands. And then he really sees his hands. They are covered in crusting blood, dry, dark flakes of it forming lines in the creases of his knuckles. And on his wrists, more blood. Some of it is brown and unlovely, but in other places it's an entrancing shade of red he can barely tear his eyes from. He feels his face and, for the first time, smells the scent of old blood there as well.

He leans over and a loud keening breaks the silence around him. The sound bounces off the empty buildings before returning to him again. His fists finally decide to obey him and he beats them against his head.

He remembers.

The beating seems to help because he remembers something else too. The memory of a young girl's fearful face shoving a square of bright, white paper through a door slot breaks through his foggy confusion. He remembers her eyes, her tears. With his more-in-control fist, he pats his jeans pocket and hears the crackling sound there.

Yes, that's right.

Find the girl. Find the girl. Find the girl.

He keeps repeating the mantra in his head as he forces his eyes away from the distractions of the birds and walks on down the road.

Today - Company at High Noon

It's a beautiful day outside, truly, epically beautiful. The sky is bright and clear blue, with just a few tiny streaks of cloud up high to make it look real. It rained last night for a good while, so everything has been washed clean. In the early light, lingering moisture glitters in shiny spots on the pavement.

And there are birds everywhere. Nests seem to be tucked into every single nook and cranny of the buildings around me. The birds flit about in the course of their errands, far more energetic than I am this morning. I'm guessing they sleep much more easily than I do at night.

The rain-washed air feels good in my lungs. I inhale a measured breath and try to envision that I'm breathing in the gorgeous day, staving off depression and loneliness by sucking in sunshine.

"Good morning, birds," I say, cheerfully.

I like to try to use my voice each day. I don't want to become one of those muttering weirdoes, but I don't want to lose my ability to speak properly either.

The birds squawk back at me, a few of them resting on the roof just above me flapping their wings indignantly and giving me the hairy eyeball. I just wave and start my rounds.

It's a bit of an irony, really. Birds are making a comeback the likes of which I doubt any book I read before all this happened ever addressed. Like almost every teenager in the country, I devoured *those* kinds of books before it all became real. I read zombie books. I read post-apocalyptic books where things went to hell because of electromagnetic pulses, wars, crazy politics, pandemics, and every other improbable situation you can imagine.

In those books, and in movies and television, all the animals make a comeback or else everything dies. There's never a middle ground. Reality, it turns out, is way different, with some clear winners and many, many losers. Birds are the winners. Squirrels, dogs, cats, and every other ground animal that I can think of offhand are the big losers.

And now, those winning birds create a daily cacophony that wakes me in the morning, accompanies me throughout the day, and warns me of approaching danger. Then, as if trying to be polite, they go quiet by degrees as the light fades so I can try to sleep.

If a deader or an in-betweener happens by during the night, individual avian voices rise and follow the movement. Sharp and insistent, those warnings wake me so that I can wait, quiet yet alert, until the danger passes. Or, if it doesn't, the birdcalls tell me exactly which way I need to go to take care of the problem.

They have it made, those birds. Not only do they sleep up high, out of reach of the metal- and blood-seeking deaders, but also because their other predators have succumbed. Cats can jump high and slink quietly, so I still see them now and again, but when they have babies they are easy targets. And a howling tomcat on the prowl is like dangling bait. You'd think the cats would have learned to be quieter when they get their groove on by now. I've not seen a kitten even once since all this happened.

I don't think it will be long before cats are gone as well. Then the birds will have this part of the world to themselves. Maybe they'll have the whole thing. I'm long past betting on humans making it to the end of this.

The complex of warehouses and light industrial buildings I live in is bordered by a fence, both strong and tall. That's why I live here, why we stopped here in the first place. It's chain link, so it provides no real attraction to the deaders. It's the wrong kind of metal, or rather, it's an alloy in which their favorite kind isn't dominant in the mix. They might attach themselves to it for a while, give it a little taste, but it doesn't seem to hold their interest for long.

Unlike the fence, some of the buildings are steel, which does attract them if they get within range. For this reason I tend to the fences with care, dragging off the deaders that I send into true death so they don't pile up against the fence and ruin my sightlines. A walk of the perimeter is always my first task and today is no exception.

A few deaders straggle along the length of my fence. All of them are in bad shape, far beyond sensing in any conventional way. One does lift its head—some dim reflex from a time when it was sighted perhaps—when I stumble on a crumbling bit of concrete and slap my boot down a little harder than I should. Its jaw moves up and down, a slow-motion mastication of air, as the nanites inside it seek to spread to a new host.

They're not easy to dispatch, but I do have a system. A quick shot with the crossbow, the *thunk* of the bolt hitting home at the base of the skull through the throat, then that stutter-step weirdness as the spinal cord is severed and the nanites try to fix things they can no longer truly fix.

That doesn't kill the deaders—even though they're dead anyway—like it does in the movies. That sort of pisses me off. By the time all this became real and fiction fell away, I was under the mistaken belief that any well-struck blow to the head would knock a deader into a less corporeal form of afterlife. I made a good many of them look like freaking porcupines I shot so many bolts into them, but still, they stutter-stepped along.

But it's all bull, and here's why. The nanites that keep the deaders ambulatory do require that the host have a functioning brain and nervous system. But only the barest, teensiest sliver of brain is actually needed. So long as some fraction of the host's mind remains connected to its body, that host will keep on moving. Even if the head and body are separated, each part will continue to survive and—if I had to guess—at least the head part will continue to suffer, for a long time.

The nanites, in carrying out their simple machine directive, maintain the host in something resembling a living state. But that same directive also requires that the nanites maintain *themselves.* To do this, they must keep building new nanites to replace those that fail or otherwise become inoperative. It's an endless, vicious circle. The nanites keep the host "alive" and craving the materials the little machines use to maintain both host and themselves. But all of it works so poorly that the result is a world gone haywire, swarming with ravenous in-betweeners and decaying deaders.

Every part of the host body teems with nanites. And true to their original designs, they can repair a lot of damage. When the host's brain or spinal cord takes a hit, the nanites go into overdrive to fix it. I've cracked heads on the driest and nastiest deaders and seen a nice, moist brain inside. That's what the nanites focus on when all else fails—the brain.

Eventually, that fails too if the host doesn't feed. Preservation of the host is the nanite directive, and just look at the mess that bit of simple computer code has brought us.

While they are busy fixing the spinal cord, it's a simple matter of walking up to the fence and poking them in enough places that they're no longer mobile. It's very messy work. If I were in medical school, I'd ace the test on where the ligaments and muscles that tie a human body together are located. Too bad for me that I wanted to be an architect and build beautiful buildings that would last the ages.

What a joke. I'm laughing. Really.

What I really need to do is smash their heads, which is very efficient and *very* final. Efficiency is good. Poking through the chain link fence is not efficient, so I just feed through a loop of wire, let it pop open, hook each deader around the neck, and tighten the loop. After that, I let the piece of pipe attached to each wire keep them stuck to the fence until I can get to them.

Once I get closer to the gate I hear the soft shuffling sounds of a larger group. It's an unmistakably creepy sound that I wouldn't have thought twice about in the past. It's probably no different from the sound of a bunch of people waiting in line at a movie theater, shuffling their feet and impatient for that weekend's blockbuster to take away their everyday worries.

The difference is that those shuffling feet always had other human sounds to cover them in the world I grew up in. Amusement-park music drowning out the sounds of the hour-long wait in line. Excited chatter and giggles covering up the pre-movie foot noises. Our crowd sounds muffled the presence of the crowd itself.

Now, it's just the birds and they are up high, avoiding contact with deaders and in-betweeners alike, exposing the sounds for what they are. And what those sounds are is danger in a form that only vaguely reminds me of their former human selves.

I'd like to just avoid this area altogether, but so much noise attracts in-betweeners. That means this spot more than any other is one I've got to keep clear. The chain link fence that surrounds this industrial complex ends at the front, where the impression needed to be a little less prison-like back when the world was normal. Along the wedge-shaped front of the complex, the chain link shifts to wrought iron fencing, the kind with fancy spikes along the top and brick pillars breaking it up every so often.

It's actually quite pretty, but unfortunately, it's also bare metal of the most attractive kind. Iron. Not cheap knock-off aluminum, not alloy, but old-school, painted wrought iron. There must be some sort of coating on it that keeps the rust at bay, but on the gate that's eroded away, leaving a rusty and attractive span of iron for the deaders to attach themselves to.

There's a good crowd of them today, at least twenty. That's a lot these days, two years into the nightmare that is our world. In the beginning, there were thousands—no, tens and hundreds of thousands—of them running around, but deaders don't last forever and they are truly, finally, dying off in droves.

I can't handle twenty by myself, but they are on the other side of the gate and most of them are in just as bad a shape as the ones from the perimeter sweep. It's almost funny, the way they look. Gross, but funny. Whatever is left of their mouths is wrapped around a rung of wrought iron, gumming away at it like teething babies with frozen teething rings.

If they sensed me nearby, they'd switch their attention to me in a heartbeat, but so long as I'm careful—and don't trip again—I should be fine with deaders this far gone. They don't speak, groan, or do any of that business. The only sounds that come from them are occasional clangs from something hitting the fence, the gooey sounds of their mouths sliding along the posts, and that ever-present soft shuffling of their feet across the pavement.

I stand there watching them a while, trying to accurately gauge the condition of each deader. Mistakes are deadly so I do try very hard not to make them.

ANN CHRISTY

People used to say that nobody is perfect, but I now think of that as an excuse for not being careful. Carefulness breeds perfection. I'm not perfect yet, as demonstrated by my tripping this morning, but I come closer each day. If there were a PhD for carefulness, I would have earned one.

Doctor Careful, thank you very much.

Something at the outer periphery of the little crowd draws my attention. It's not anything big or obvious, but there's purpose somewhere there in the movements. An in-betweener? Two steps backward brings me even with the back of a truck. It's parked neatly along the side of the access road where it has been since that first bad day. Orderly stacks of orange cones meant to alert motorists fill the bed of the truck, still waiting patiently for someone to arrange them on a street somewhere. They make for even better cover.

I duck behind the truck, but slowly and without sudden movements that could attract even the dimmest-sighted deader. Peering from between the pointed barriers of the stacked cones, I examine each head carefully. I can't see past the deaders particularly well, but I'm patient and eventually I'm rewarded for my patience.

The in-betweener is a newly minted one. The only part of him that I can really see is from the forehead up, but the neat haircut and the general shape of his head tells me he's a man, one who joined the ranks of in-betweeners very recently.

After a long while listening to their gushy licking noises, the in-betweener finally makes an appearance by moving to the side, away from the gate. He walks toward the area where the brick bottom and pillars make reaching the iron more difficult

26

for the deaders. He's tall and very close to living, his color only pale and not any of the more colorful shades the deaders progress through over time.

His clothes are dirty, but still recognizable. His hair is still brown and unmatted by time and the environment. The rain may have cleaned him up a bit, but the overall impression I get from him is someone recently made into an in-betweener. There are stains on the pale blue over-shirt he's wearing that cover the arms from wrist to elbow. I'm thinking blood.

He reaches out with dirty hands toward the bars, stretching a little to get past the substantial brick base. I've measured it in the past, and the foundation is three feet thick and three feet high. That's enough to keep a car from crashing through, but not so high as to be unattractive. The ironwork bars of the fence extend upward from that.

At first, he seems a little confused, like he can't understand why he wants the iron bars and knows he's forgetting something—probably the sight of me. Eventually he settles, strokes one of the bars a little, and leans forward awkwardly to wrap his lips around it. His eyes don't close, but I can tell he's content. That's how they get, sort of content, when they satisfy an imperative. Obtaining iron is an imperative. The closest thing to a look of happiness I've ever seen on them is when they get hold of a cell phone or some other electronic device, especially if it's busted up. All those rare metals, you know. Still, he looks content now with his iron bar.

He's young, probably not much older than me. Maybe he was a college student or recently graduated. The way he's dressed—the jeans and the T-shirt with a button-up shirt over it as a sort of jacket—speaks student to me. Maybe a grad student?

I look him over and finally see what took him from regular human to in-betweener. There's a neat hole in his T-shirt, right above a beer logo, and the brown of old blood is now visible against the dark green of the cotton. Someone shot him. I wonder why. Was he trying to steal someone's food? Or woman? Or was he protecting something—or someone—that another person wanted?

I'll never know, I don't guess, but it's good information nonetheless. It tells me that there are sufficient people and resources nearby to provide regular changes of clothes, haircuts, shaving materials—and the time and safety to be concerned with shaving—and weapons. That's not good.

Unfortunately, in exchange for that information, I'm now stuck where I am. Between me and the buildings is the access road and he will see me clear as day if I try to cross. There's no other viable way to go unless I try to crawl backward, keeping the ever-decreasing relative size of the truck between me and him. It's at least a few hundred feet until I get to the curve in the access road that circles the entire complex. Encumbered as I am, that will take a while. And he's too far away for me to shoot with the kind of accuracy I would need. And that's not even taking into account the difficulty of trying to aim through the bars of the fence while the target is moving. I'm good, but not that good.

I decide to wait him out a little. In-betweeners are generally fickle. Their attention is easily diverted because their imperatives are so varied. By the time they become deaders, their goals are reduced to spreading to new hosts and finding stationary sources of metals they can use.

Deaders don't really fight at that point, but they do want to get their mouths on you and break the skin. In groups, their individual weakness is overcome by sheer mass and momentum. It's easy to get overwhelmed if you wind up surrounded. No one can ever say they aren't persistent when they have prey nearby, only that they're fickle when there's no prey to be found. It's super-inconvenient, that's for sure.

And once deaders get their mouths on something with a pulse, sometimes they keep going, reverting to the more aggressive in-betweener behavior. I've seen it happen. Not as often anymore because there aren't that many living things available, but I know the drill.

The most recent such attack, at least that I've seen, was on a dog that somehow managed to survive out here on the outskirts of town. I was trying to get to the dog as well, but not for food. I wanted him to keep me company. In truth, I'd been desperate for him, but he was wary and wouldn't come near me. He'd learned that not everything that looked human was human. But I'm patient in all things, including winning over a wary dog that looked like he could really use a good meal of spam.

A deader surprised me by coming out of the woods surrounding this complex and going straight for the dog. I'd yelled from my place behind my fence, told the dog to shoo, eventually screaming and crying, but all that did was confuse the dog and keep his wary eyes on me instead of behind him, where he might have seen the danger.

I don't want to see any more dogs.

In-betweeners, on the other hand, *always* crave the material that will rebuild their injuries and keep them going. Their nanites don't know that their host is really already dead. Nanites aren't sentient or anything. They just know their program and their program is to repair damage to their hosts and themselves.

And what better source of the rich proteins, amino acids, and other building blocks of animal life is there but another animal? Our iron-rich blood by itself is enough to make them want to attack, but our organs are the real prize. Meat, especially dead meat, is a distant third, but they'll go for it if it's around. Except deader meat for some reason. That doesn't interest them.

It's a nice day out, which is weird in a way. I sort of feel like beautiful weather is almost an insult when everything else is such a mess, but today it's on my side. I manage to get myself seated behind the truck without making noise and get comfortable. Then I just watch the in-betweener.

After watching for a good while, I realize that I'm absently fingering the scar that runs almost all the way around the side of my skull, creating a permanent part in my hair that only shows when I pull it back into a ponytail. When my hair is pulled back like that, the streak of white scalp stands out against my black hair like a flag. It used to draw people's eyes to the line that runs from above my ear to the back of my head, a look of curious pity almost always rising on their faces. It almost looks as if someone once tried to crack open the top of my head like a can of soup.

In a way, something did try to do just that. Medulloblastoma, stage IV. It's the reason I almost died and the reason I'm still alive. My mother never would have gotten so interested in nanites without medulloblastoma, so it's a weird relationship I have with my brain.

I pull my hand away from my head and force it into my lap. After more waiting, the warm breeze starts to feel good and the shaded light creates a sort of haven of comfort right where I sit on the hard pavement. It's possibly stupid, and I know it even as I settle back against the ground with my empty backpacks as a pillow, but I decide that I need the light and the vitamin D. In reality, it's probably safer to doze here and let him wander off. Besides, dozing isn't *really* sleeping, is it?

Six Years Ago - My Medullo and Me

"You know why, Emily," my mother says.

Her eyes leave mine and she looks at the wrist she's been stroking with gentle mother touches as she speaks. I look too. The skin is thin, abnormally so, and the blue lines of my veins are so visible and clear that it seems the stroking alone might be enough to break them wide open. Given the situation, I'd almost favor that happening. My head hurts so bad I want to bang it on something, or stop breathing.

"I don't *want* any more treatments. I just want it to end. I want to stop having cancer and if I can't, then I want to stop cancer from hurting me anymore." I say it quickly and I hate how weak my voice sounds.

My mother's hand comes to a stop on my arm, her fingers resting near the latest IV. For what I'm about to do, my port isn't enough. I need more points of entry into my body, more needles.

"Don't say that. Don't ever say that," she whispers, her voice urgent.

I've never said anything like that before and it scares her. I'm agreeable because I've always been lost as to what else to say except, "Okay."

I'm no doctor and I never cared a bit about medical stuff. I'm twelve and most of what I read about medulloblastoma scares me half to death. Why would I have cared about that before I got sick? And after my diagnosis I was curious, but my mom screened everything. No blogs by dying kids for me. No playdates with the other terminals. And no medical websites, ever.

She looks around the hospital room, even though there's no one in here except the two of us. It's as if she's afraid that whoever authorized my upcoming treatment will change their mind if they hear me say I'm sick of being sick. I'm sick of *dying*. But I think anyone who deals with people dying of cancer every day would understand how I feel. Only someone who has been healthy their whole life wouldn't get it. I've had this since I was nine years old. That's a long time.

"I'm sorry," I say, relenting at the hurt look on her face.

She nods, her face worried and her lips tight with the fear she won't admit she carries around inside her. Otherwise, she looks no different than any other day. Her uniform is perfect, as usual, but even that can't erase the fact that she's not a Marine right now, she's a mom in full mom-mode.

She takes a deep breath and then tilts my chin up toward her, so I'll have to look at her or try really hard not to. As always, she focuses only on my left eye because that's the one that works. My right eye doesn't sit correctly in its socket and my sight is all but gone in it. My tumor is big and there's just no room in my head now. Her eyes flit once toward the giant pink scar on my bald head, but return to my eye again. Her two sighted eyes are filled with love.

"I know you're tired, baby girl. There's just one more hurdle to get through. This is going to work. Have I ever made that promise before? I'm making it now. This is going to work and you *will* get better."

There's a light in her eyes that's almost frightening. It's fervent and desperate. For a moment, I'm convinced that her life is tied to mine, that she'll die when I do. And I know I will die. I know it like I know that tonight they'll give me something to "relax" me and then wake me at least three times to check my vitals while I try to sleep, ensuring that I don't relax at all. This thing we're doing is a pipe dream.

We both startle as the door opens abruptly and two doctors stride in. They have white coats, but their camouflaged trousers showing below the hems give them away as military. One is sporting blue camis, while the other is wearing a sort of muddled tan cami pattern similar to my mother's.

Blue Cami doctor says, "Hello there, Emily. I'm Doctor Reed. We're here to walk you through the procedure for tomorrow. Is this a good time?"

My mother stands, her posture straight and her hands curled into loose fists at her sides. I know that posture. It's called standing at attention and my mom doesn't do that often, I don't think. She wears silver oak leaves on her dressier uniforms and I thought that was a pretty high rank. It actually makes me nervous that she feels she has to remain at attention for these doctors.

Tan Cami doctor gives her a little downward wave and she sags a bit, her hands once more twisting at her waist and the strain deepening the lines of her face.

"Of course," she says.

I nod because both doctors look at me, seeming to expect an answer from me as well.

Tan Cami doctor eyes my mother again and then suggests, "Why don't we all take a seat and get as comfortable as we can."

Mom squeezes next to me on the bed, her hand finding my wrist again, while the two doctors drag over seats. My room is very big and strangely empty. I think that this room is meant to house a lot of machines based on all the ports and connections all over the walls, but for now, it's just big and empty feeling.

"Okay, first things first," Blue Cami says. "This procedure is far more straightforward than anything you've been through so far. I'd like to get that out of the way first. The surgical pain will be minimal."

When I breathe in, I can feel the air catching painfully the whole way down and tears fill my eyes. He sees the hitching of my chest and reaches out to touch my blanket-covered foot. He gives it a firm squeeze that is so compassionate I immediately know I'll go along with whatever comes next without complaint.

He taps his tablet and an image of my head comes up. It's not pretty. His fingers make patterns on the glass and the image changes from photo to internal views, first my scarred-up skull, then on to the inside where all the bad stuff is—as well as the brain that makes me who I am. Or it did until the tumor got so big I began to lose even that. With my failing memory—people and places I loved are gone, replaced by scary blank spots—and the increasingly frequent seizures, I'm less myself with each passing day.

Soon enough, the mass that is my tumor takes up the bulk of the image, my brain a ghostly shadow around it. The tumor is mushed up, like even *it* is getting squeezed by the tight confines of my skull, bulging in some areas, stretched and thin in others. And through it all, I see once again why tumors like mine are so hard to simply cut out. It threads through my gray matter like ribbons.

The image begins to move—an animation of some sort— and Blue Cami taps the sharp object now pointed at the bones of my head. "This," he says, "is where we're going to drill a small entry hole for insertion." Another tap on the screen and the pointed object moves back, a small tube replacing it. "And this is the only thing we'll need to use inside. Here, you can see what it will look like."

He holds the tablet still so I can really see what happens. Out of the small tube comes a very tiny pointed object. It does look exceedingly small compared to my head, maybe the size of one of those red plastic stirrers used for coffee. At my expression, Tan Cami says, "That's a small-bore needle in the most basic terms."

I nod absently and keep watching. The tiny needle pierces the mass that lives inside me and slows down, burrowing farther inside. At the far end of the main mass, it stops and a tiny stream of silver flows out to form a small bubble. After that short pause, it pulls back, leaving a trail of silver that looks like snail slime in sunlight in its wake. Then it does the same thing on the other side of the mass. Then, without ceremony—or taking a bow—the tube withdraws and the animation is over.

"That's it?" my mother and I ask at the same time.

Both doctors smile at that. Blue Cami puts away the tablet and says, "We'll put a small plug into the hole to keep your skull from closing for now, but it will be very small. That's in case we need to insert more of our little friends later. Then a few stitches on your scalp, but nothing like what you've had to endure so far."

I can't even imagine it. I've had three brain surgeries, one of which took out a plate of bone big enough to be troublesome because it wouldn't heal properly when it was replaced. So yeah, I'd say I've been through the wringer already. A tiny hole? I can deal with that.

But will it work? I don't believe it. Not really.

How many of us died while they were developing this cure? Why should I get so lucky that this treatment gets approved for testing now, right when I'm at the end of the road? Are these "little friends"—these tiny nanomachines called Medulloblastoma Digesting Nanites (MBDNs)—really going to save me or will they eat my brain instead?

The cold hard fact is that no one knows. I'm one of the first patients included in this experimental study, thanks to a compassionate-use exception my mother fought to get me at the risk of her career and our health insurance. But she won and I'm sitting in front of the two men who may save my life. Or, put machines into my head that will devour my brain.

I suppose, either way it goes, I'll get my wish. It will be over once and for all. Either no cancer or no brain. I'll take it.

"I'm ready," I say.

Today - The Speaker

"Garah! Garah da!" I hear as I wake up, sweaty and uncomfortable on the pavement. My head is pounding out a monotonous *bang bang* in time with my heart. I've also moved in my sleep and I can see straight through to the wrought iron fence and the in-betweener standing there.

The voice. Where did that come from? Reality or dream? I reach for the crossbow next to me, but then change my mind and reach for the rifle instead. Voices mean people and I'm not taking chances. If that voice was real, that is.

"Garah!"

The voice is a bit off and reminds me of the way some deaf people speak, forming words based only on the way the mouth and throat move rather than the nuances of sound. I get up and crouch behind the truck, trying to see in every direction at once. I could swear the voice was coming from the direction of the fence, but the deaders are still gumming their way along the iron so there couldn't be a person there. If there were a person there, they would be focusing on him or her.

"Garah da! Oda ha!"

Then I see it. The voice *does* belong to the in-betweener, and he's looking in my direction, his hand wavering between being raised in a wave and shaking downward without direction. He seems to be fighting himself, looking off at other things and then jerking back toward me. It seems like he's working really hard at it too.

Which is weird because, well, because he's a reanimated corpse or something very close to it. Maybe revived corpse would be a better description.

They don't talk.

"Garah kahm. Garah, garah. Ged garah!" he says, almost yelling the words and jerking his head forward in emphasis with each repetition. His face twists into something that looks so much like human desperation that I get a flash of my mother's face when I was at my sickest in my head.

A couple of the deaders lift their heads at his latest outburst, heads bouncing unsteadily as they try to work out if there's something they should be interested in. One of them breaks away from the gate and stumbles along the fence toward the in-betweener. He jerks a little to the side, watching the deader, and his face twists into a new expression. This time I can see what it means without doubt of any kind. It's disgust.

Once the deader gets within reach of him, it stops, perhaps sensing that this potential new host is already hosting his own complement of nanites and not in need of more. But it still stands there, weaving back and forth.

The in-betweener takes a few, remarkably human-looking steps toward the deader. Very abruptly, he reaches out and twists the deader's head. I can hear the bones crunch and grind all the way from behind the truck where I watch events unfold.

Almost immediately, the jerky nanite overdrive starts in the deader. While it flounders, the in-betweener drags it over to a car lying half in the ditch outside the gate and tosses it in, slamming the door behind it. All the action and the loud sound of the car door causes another ripple of interest from the deaders at the gate, but it passes quickly.

All I can do is squat there, gape at the in-betweener, and clutch at my rifle like it's a security blanket. Am I wrong about him being an in-betweener? I've never seen one doing this much in a purposeful way before. I've certainly never seen them speak. New ones do make noise, unlike the deaders, but nothing organized that I've ever seen. Then again, I don't see them much because I hole up here. I don't go looking for them.

Maybe they are all like that. Maybe they have card games and movie nights and organize weird raves where the party drugs are humans instead of pills. I don't frigging know. But I do know what I just saw and, even though he wasn't as coordinated as I might have been, what he just did was an entirely human set of actions.

He comes back to the fence and seems more like an in-betweener for a moment. He touches the rails and his mouth opens like he's going to start licking at it again, but then he stops, shakes his head, and surprises me by hitting himself. Not a tap or a slap or anything like that. He slugs himself in the head with his fist, hard, like maybe he's angry that he's strayed from his purpose.

"Garah," he yells again, but this time there's a heartbreaking note of pleading in it.

I peek out quickly to see what the deaders are doing. Now, they seem agitated by what's going on, so there's no way I'm going to give them a target to fixate on. And I'm not stupid enough to trust an in-betweener. They are dangerous because of what they are and they eat people.

Before I can stop myself, I pull myself fully behind the truck and call out, "What do you want?"

"Garah kahm. Kads! Kads!" he yells out immediately.

"I can't understand you," I return, telling myself that I'm an idiot that is about to get herself killed by falling for some new form of in-betweener party trick.

He doesn't answer right away so I peek out, fully expecting to see him climbing the fence and ready to have himself a little Emily-flavored snack. Instead, I see him holding his head in both hands and bending over a little. He straightens after a moment, grips the fence with one fist and pokes the other hand through the rails. He extends a finger in my direction—I can see that his hand is shaking violently with the strain of it—and says, "Garah. Ya garah."

I still don't get it, but he doesn't wait for confirmation because his hand twists into the universal sign that means "come here" and he says, "Kahm."

Okay, that one I get. He wants me to come, something which is *so* not going to happen.

Again, he doesn't wait. His face is screwed up in intense concentration and he lowers his hand, turning it so that it faces palm down, until it is as low as he can get it given the brick base of the wall, and says, "Kads."

That seems to be it for his message, because his hand moves back toward his side of the fence and the pleading look is on his face again. He can't really see me well since I'm peeking from behind the bumper of a truck, but he's waiting. There is hope all over his pale face.

I lean back and think. Come, I get. He wants me to come. What about the pointing finger and the *Ya garah*. I turn the words around in my head, changing the inflections and trying to think of the way that deaf schoolmate of mine said her words. The pointing finger was toward me. Then I realize what it means. He's saying, "You girl." He kept repeating the *garah* word over and over, *girl, girl, girl*.

Figuring that word out helps me to understand his final sign almost immediately. *Kads* means kids. The hand set about waist height, the desperate face. This in-betweener wants me to come and help some kids. But, why? Wouldn't he rather just eat them?

I look back from around the truck with a new understanding and a whole slew of new fears. First, there's the uncharacteristic behavior to fear. Second is the idea that an in-betweener is trying to get help for someone else, and third is the very real possibility that if he can do that much complex thinking, he could also be lying in order to get a fresh meal.

He's just standing there, both fists tight around the fence and his arms locked straight, like he's trying to force himself *not* to start licking the tempting metal in front of him. And it is very tempting. There's metal everywhere, but good old iron is a favorite of theirs. Maybe they feel about iron the way I feel about cheese curls. They haunt my dreams sometimes. Bags and bags of them just out of reach. I could tear up some cheese curls right about now, two years past the expiration date or not.

Enough dreaming about the cheese curls. Thinking about that is just torture and I'm avoiding the fact that I know what he's trying so hard to communicate to me. I do that sometimes, avoid thinking about hard stuff by dreaming of something else. It's a bad habit. I take a deep breath and grip my rifle tightly in my suddenly sweaty fists.

"You have kids somewhere that need help. Is that what you're saying?" I call out and hear a relieved groan in response.

"Are they human?" I ask, then cringe when I realize what I'm asking and to whom I'm asking the question.

He doesn't react to that in a negative way at all, but rather he bounces on his knees, as if excited by my question. "Yah!"

"Bring them here," I call out. I'm not leaving this compound, but kids, especially waist-high ones, make it impossible for me to simply walk away.

He shakes his head violently and mumbles something I can't understand.

"Are there more of you? Is that why you can't?" I ask.

The bouncing knees commence again and I understand suddenly that this is his way of nodding. And I understand what the problem is. If there is some part of him that wants to save those kids, then that part also knows he can't herd kids in his state. Perhaps he realizes that he can't be trusted with them.

I have to think about this. My only goals for today were to walk the perimeter and clear off any deaders, grab some food from the distribution warehouse inside the complex, and get a little sunshine to stave off depression. That's it.

I don't leave the complex except to dispatch my fence deaders, and even then I rarely go more than a hundred feet from the fence. The last time I truly left was more than a year ago, before my mom died and was reborn, the fever that killed her leaving her red-faced and puffy, the nanites that restarted her heart leaving her brain-damaged and dangerous. Then, I'd left seeking medicine and hadn't found anything useful. There's no reason to leave now.

Except, maybe there is.

"Shit," I say softly to the bumper of the truck.

Five Years Ago - Magic Beans for Everyone

On the screen, a man is wheeled out in a wheelchair. At his appearance, flashbulbs pop from somewhere off camera in a rapid, dizzying fire. He sends a nervous glance toward the camera, but seems to collect himself as the woman pushing his chair brings it to a stop and locks its wheels. Her arm brushes his shoulder as she steps back a little, sending a bit of surreptitious comfort his way.

He must be getting cues from someone off screen, because he nods at somebody, grits his teeth, and then awkwardly stands up from his wheelchair. Under normal circumstances, a man rising from a chair wouldn't be significant, but when he does it, a round of applause greets him. It's so intense that the TV has to adjust the sound down to avoid exceeding our maximum comfortable set point.

The row of doctors sitting at the press conference table stand as well, their applause for the man who is standing rather than for themselves, but it is they who have created the miracle. The man is unsteady and his smiling attendant holds his elbow firmly to keep him from losing his balance.

One of those doctors is Blue Cami. His name is Doctor Reed, but he lets me call him by the name I used when I had trouble remembering names at all, sometimes even my own. He calls me Rat in return. I earned that name. I used to accuse him of using me as a lab rat when he was working to cure me with his brand-new nanites. And he did cure me.

Now he's working on yet another set of neurological nanomachines. That's his specialty and it looks like he's got another winner.

The standing man turns his head and gives his attendant a look, a cue for her to help him back into his chair. As he sits and the fabric of the cotton pants he wears tightens around his legs, I can see how thin his legs are. They're wasted from lack of mobility and trembling a little from the effort of standing.

Behind the doctors, a large video screen showing only the hospital logo suddenly flares into more colorful life and displays an image of the man in the wheelchair as he was before his nanite-created miracle. The contrast between the image and the man as he is now is startling. In the image, he has a tube coming out of his throat and a band across his forehead. The chair he sits in is more support structure than actual chair, and he appears to be entirely helpless.

Because he *was* entirely helpless. Paralyzed from the neck down to such catastrophic extent that he couldn't even breathe on his own or hold his own head up. And he'd been like that for over a year.

I watch the rest of the press conference in rapt attention. My hair has grown back but my fingers still follow the path of the scar beneath the hair that hides it from view. Or, rather, hides it most of the time. Like me, the man in the wheelchair has been cured by very specialized nanites.

His nanites were different, of course, but the effect is the same. A cure. A repair. A recovery of something that had been lost. In my case, I recovered my hope for a long life. In his case, he recovered his ability to feel his own body. His spinal nerve has been repaired and, while he shyly acknowledges that he has a long road to recovery, he is equally confident that it will happen, as are the doctors.

His is not the first press conference. Because of our ages, I and most of the other children who benefited from the same procedure I underwent were not paraded in front of cameras like this man. But one girl, so radiantly happy that she almost glowed, had spoken for all of us on an earlier occasion.

I'd watched that conference too, that time holding my mother's hand with a patch over my right eye. This time, I watch the man, his excited family, and the doctors, but now I can see them with both of my eyes. My right eye isn't perfect—too much nerve damage—but I can now see well enough with it that I'm grateful. And if it wanders off kilter now and then, well, that's not such a high price to pay.

Besides, Blue Cami says that nanites specializing in the repair of optic nerves are a few years away at most. I say it will be before then. The senses are too important for those to fall low on the priority list. I'd be willing to bet on that. I can wait for them. I'm alive and I can wait a few years. It still feels unreal to think that sometimes.

I have time. Glorious, wonderful, mysterious time.

Since my cure, the thousands of children who once felt life slipping away from their grasp as medulloblastoma grew inside their skulls have regained their hope for life. Very few suffer complications and almost none of them die.

As one of the first to receive this treatment, my biggest problem was how much gunk built up in my cerebrospinal fluid as my tumor got digested away. They do it more slowly now. For my second treatment, they fed the nanites in over a period of hours, right into my spinal fluid rather than through my skull. I watched TV during the procedure and didn't feel a thing. My mother says that my kind of cancer is very close to being almost entirely curable.

And now this man joins our nanite-cured throngs. And we're not alone. Along with us for this miracle ride are those who once suffered from several other types of tumor, a few kinds of liver disease, and a host of bacterial infections. They've even got a nanite for sickle-cell anemia.

There is no single cure-all, but it seems that every day a new form of tiny machine is created that will resolve some other vexing or dangerously life-threatening problem. Everyone, everywhere is making them. That's where the research money flows to now. And it is flowing hard and fast.

I call them my magic beans. Soon there will be magic beans for everyone.

Today - The Loneliness of Being Alive

I should be thinking about the danger of a talking in-betweener or the danger of any trip outside my complex. I should be recommitting myself to avoiding any creature that isn't a deader in need of meeting its maker. Let's face it, even entertaining such an idea is how people lose their PhDs in Caution. Instead, all I can think of is companionship in the form of these unknown children.

Survival is a desperately lonely business. Trust is not achievable in any real way once a catastrophe of this magnitude happens. You can only trust those you already know and, even then, maybe not always, maybe not entirely. Unless they're your mom, that is. The bonds of love—like those between my mother and me—were what I could trust, but not anyone or anything else. It can make a person start talking to themselves in a way that's not entirely healthy.

I'm not even really thinking of the kids as people in need of saving in the altruistic way I might have before all this happened. That's there, of course, but it is threaded through with the wondrous idea of someone to talk to, to interact with, to hear breathing during the long nights so that I know I'm not alone. My heartbeat kicks up a notch as the idea catches hold inside me. I push a breath out through my puffed-up cheeks.

Keep it together, I think. *Excitement can make you lose your focus just as quickly as fear.*

It works. The little thrill in my chest eases back a bit as I run through a mental list of everything that can go wrong. Always have a plan and form that plan based on the best information you can get. That's my motto and I'm going with it.

First things, first. There is an in-betweener with a bullet hole in his chest who is speaking to me. And I have no idea where he came from and how long he'll be able to maintain this level of coherent behavior. Like I said before, they are notoriously unpredictable. Easily distracted, but no less dangerous.

Peeking back out from around the bumper, I see him still standing at the fence, his fists tight around the rails and his eyes steadily on the truck. The strain on his face is obvious. He's really trying.

"Where are they?" I ask, with little hope that he'll be able to convey anything detailed like that, but asking anyway.

He jerks, his jaws working in the way I'm more familiar with when it comes to in-betweeners. The concentration of before leaves his face and an eager sort of searching replaces it. My heart sinks at that, but then he surprises me again by banging his head against the fence hard enough to make it clang.

Fresh, new blood mars his forehead when he pulls back. That's a good sign in a way. It means his nanites restarted his heart quickly enough that his blood is still flowing well and circulating, becoming oxygenated and then providing that oxygen to his body. Given his actions, I'm thinking he's more like a brain-damaged human with decent functioning and some obvious measure of control.

He's back on task again, the momentary lapse into in-betweener-ness over. His hand is jerky and uncoordinated and he misses the first time he tries to jam it into his pocket, but on the second try he manages to extract a piece of paper. He pushes it through the bars, holds it for a few seconds, and then lets it go. It flutters in the light breeze, the folds coming undone so that it flaps like a bird or a poorly made paper airplane. As it moves along the grass away from me, I see panic in his face.

The last thing I want is to come out of my hiding place and into plain view of either the in-betweener or the group of deaders. The deaders can't climb over a fence, but they can get agitated and that draws others. The in-betweener is more than capable of climbing a fence. This whole situation has been one long risk and I'm pushing things.

"Dammit," I grumble to my friend, the truck bumper. Before I can think any more about it, I drop everything except my rifle, get to my feet, and sprint across the road and into the big grassy area that fronts the complex.

The paper flutters with more energy as the breeze picks up momentarily and I lose it behind the big sign that tells visitors the name of the complex. I pass by the in-betweener without giving him a direct look, but out of the corner of my eye I see him lose focus and snap his jaws in in-betweener mode again.

That makes me put my head down and push my legs harder. I'm not used to this sort of full-on effort anymore. I spend my time being quiet and careful, which generally also means slow. This kind of running is almost alien to my body after all this time. It feels good, even though I'm terrified.

I catch sight of the paper again as it scoots along the overgrown grass and veer so I'll intersect its path. The grass is taller farther into the green space, coming up to my knees and matted with last year's dead stems. I almost take a header into it when I risk a glance backward just to make sure the in-betweener is still on his side of the fence. He is, but he's agitated and I can tell it won't be long until he makes a move. My running is just exciting him.

Then I'll have to stop and kill him again. I just hope the paper has all the information I need if it comes to that.

The paper almost gets away from me one more time, but I finally grab it when it dips into some tall grass. As soon as I'm sure I have it, I drop down and use that same tall grass as cover. The in-betweener seems to be battling himself at the moment, walking in circles and hitting himself in the head. Some of the deaders sense the disturbance and pause in their fence licking, while the rest continue on as before, oblivious.

Slinging the rifle onto my lap so that it's in just the right position to pick up and fire, I greedily open the note. It's spattered with brown drops of dried blood, and some that seem fresher, but the writing is legible. Some part of me is filled with excitement at the very idea of opening a paper written by another hand, even while the rest of me fears what I'll read, and how that might change the trajectory of my career in professional caution.

The handwriting is young, busy with big looping letters and circles instead of dots over the letters that need such. I run my hand over it before I can even read it, the indirect touch of another person almost overwhelming me for a second or two. One more look at the in-betweener and I read:

Hello! The man with this note is Sam and he won't hurt you if you are careful. He was a teacher and he takes care of us, but then he got shot by accident. I timed it and he was gone for three minutes so he's not as bad as most. But he is not doing well and we sent him to find you before something bad happens. He watched you but we didn't get a chance to come to where you are. There are five of us but Penny and Jon are little and I can only carry one of them. Please come and find us. He can bring you but if not, here is our address. Love, Veronica

P.S. If you feed him animals he isn't as dangerous.

Below that, the girl had drawn a row of hearts and noted their address. An address I don't know at all. An address I *know* I will find.

Four Years Ago - A Life Saved Is a Future Saved

"**D**eath from sudden heart attack may be a thing of the past!" the newscaster announces with a wide grin that speaks to me of a love of cheeseburgers. So I say that out loud.

My mother snorts and taps at her tablet, immersed in some bit of work that's followed her home. Her fingernail makes a series of rapid clicks against the glass of the tablet, and then she makes a little noise of satisfaction. Another problem solved.

What my mother does in the military has nothing to do with fighting—at least I don't think so—and everything to do with computer programming. That just means she's always busy. For her, the fight is twenty-four hours a day and seven days a week. She works at home every night and every weekend. She loves her job, though, so there's that.

I turn up the TV a little to cover the sound of her taps. This is one bit of news I want to listen to.

This new nanite is a doozy and probably deserves a little excitement. Finding the cure-all nanite isn't likely, but more and different kinds of nanites are now available to mix and match as the need arises. This particular type can be administered by emergency responders. It can restart the heart and fix heart tissue, rendering the heart normal again after the worst has happened. They're calling them First Responders. I wonder how the real first responders of the world—namely, the firefighters and paramedics—feel about a bunch of nanites being given their name.

It's true that most people won't get that far down the road of heart failure. Anyone with clogged arteries is receiving injections of the plaque-eating nanites, but sometimes things just happen. I'll bet there are a million sighs of relief coming from a million chests right about now.

After a moment of listening to the news anchor gushing on about these new nanites, my mother says, "Well, this is good news for the transfat people."

I laugh and answer, "Well, there's no transfat in ice cream, but it's got loads of saturated fat. Can I have some?"

She looks up from her tablet and winks. "Only if you get me some too."

We eat ice cream and watch the extended coverage of this new advance. Nanites are great, but they aren't computationally complex enough to do many different things. They are purpose built.

Artery-clearing nanites travel the bloodstream, using pincers and jaws to remove plaque from cholesterol buildup. Others are engineered to digest other compounds or grab onto cells much larger than themselves and simply burst them, rendering them unable to carry out their biological imperatives. It's complicated, but exciting.

A new segment comes on, this one very different from the upbeat tenor of the previous program, the tone this time far more serious. Gushing, cheeseburger-loving anchors are replaced by the serious faces of the typical older anchor and an expert guest.

"But, and this is a big issue, Troy, we'd be remiss if we didn't examine the potential dangers," the newscaster says.

To me, it looks like the expert is about ready to jump out of his chair and start waving his hands like those crazy people on the street corners always warning us about the end of the world. The newscaster barely finishes speaking before he jumps in.

"This is new technology, one in which the long-term impacts to health are entirely unknown," he begins. He sounds reasonable, but excited in the way people who have bad news they can't wait to share are. I can almost hear the movie music signaling impending doom in the background. "New nanites are coming out too fast for anything like the extensive testing we really need. And people are loading up on every kind of nanite, with no thought to how many different types they've got inside them and what might happen as a result."

"Hey, Mom. Listen to this for a minute," I say, putting my empty bowl of ice cream on the coffee table.

She looks up, then back down at her tablet, then at me. I know she's trying to decide if work can wait, so I smile and point at the screen. That does the trick, because she puts her work aside and tucks her feet up under my blanket on the couch, all her attention now on the screen.

The newscaster is one I'm not particularly fond of. When he's trying to be serious he always draws his face down in a frown so severe that it makes his facelift look weird, like it's too tight or something.

He nods sagely at the expert's words, then asks, "Even if that were true, don't the nanites simply do their work, go inactive, and then get flushed out of the system? Should people be afraid and then pass up the chance for a longer and healthier life? Isn't that overly cautious, even alarmist?"

The expert shakes his head. "You make it sound like it's an either-or situation when it isn't," the fellow shoots back, his irritation showing. "What I'm saying is that the current trend is to have nanites injected even when there's no viable medical need. In particular, there's a huge underground trade in cheap knock-off plaque nanites. Millions of people around the world, some as young as their twenties, are getting pumped full of nanites without a diagnosis or prescription. Young people whose arteries are almost certainly clean as a whistle are loading up on these things—all for no better reason than 'just in case.' Using a radically new and only minimally tested technology in this way is downright foolhardy."

The newscaster nods again, giving the old wise-man imitation he's known for. He says, "I don't think anyone is encouraging irresponsible medical treatments, whether nanite-based or not. But you have to admit…"

I tune them out at that point, a thought coming to me.

"Mom, do you have nanites?" I ask.

She starts at that, then picks at the fringe at the edge of the blanket. I know my answer already.

"I do, but not like what that man is talking about," she says, waving toward the TV and the talking heads.

I think that's sort of funny, because she was very insistent about ensuring all my nanites left my system once my tumor was gone. I figured she was creeped out by the idea of me having machines inside me and here she is, adding them to her own bloodstream.

"What kind?"

She laughs. "Oh, well, the same ones everyone's got now, I'd guess."

"Which ones? The artery ones?"

She nods and smiles, but she's examining my face for my reaction.

I'm not sure what I think of that. Mostly, I wonder if that means she had something wrong with her. There's no denying that my associations with nanites lead me to think of them as the things that bring us back from the brink of death.

My mom must see something of this in my face, because she reaches out to tuck a strand of hair behind my ear and says, "I'm not sick, sweetie. I had a little build-up in my arteries from all that ship food and a lifetime of ice cream, but the nanites went in and did their stuff. I'm sure they're probably gone by now. It was just a shot at the doctor's office. Nothing more."

I take that in and look back at the muted screen, the talking heads still in full debate. The remote lies on the arm of the couch, so I pick it up and click off the program.

My mom is still looking at me, waiting for me to say whatever it is I'd like to say.

"That's cool, Mom. I want you to stick around forever. We can be all nanited up together."

She laughs and picks my ice cream bowl up off the coffee table, holding it out for me.

"Then more ice cream is definitely called for. My pipes are all clean now," she says.

I take our bowls and go into the kitchen, scooping rocky road from the carton and listening to my mother tap away on her tablet, her break over.

The expert's words still twist about in my mind. We were so careful with my nanites. Granted, they were primitive compared to those being manufactured now, just two years later, but still. It does seem odd that people would just buy cheap knock-offs from who knows where and put them inside their bodies. They could be hacked, or carry malicious code or something. Everyone knows the country that provides most of our cheaper electronics always plants code in everything they make. Even toasters!

I suppose people risk it because the fear of death is so strong, probably the strongest fear humans have. With good reason. We'll do almost anything to avoid dying. I suppose this shouldn't surprise me. I, of all people, should know how far someone will go to live.

Shrugging off the expert's words, I make a point of looking at the positive side of this. Advances are being made every single day in the new wonderland that is medical nanite technology. By the time I'm old enough to worry about things like heart attacks, I won't have to worry about them at all.

I like that idea. Another bowl of ice cream sounds like a perfect way to celebrate.

Today - In Between You and Me

In typical in-betweener fashion, the recently deceased guy at the fence seems to have lost interest in finding me, perhaps forgetting that I'm here at all. I study him with a new perspective from my hidden spot in the tall grass. I now know his name and at least a little of his past.

He's a revived dead person—meaning his nanites restarted his heart and closed up major wounds—but he *was* dead. And dead for three minutes means massive brain damage. That's what makes him an in-betweener. Not dead and not alive, merely functioning.

Yet, somehow, despite all of that, he is still trying to protect some children who aren't even his. Out of all the things he might remember, that is what he's holding onto. I figured that some memories might remain, but still, this is heartbreaking. They must have known I was here all this time and simply left me alone because…well…because people are dangerous.

More than likely, they—or he—didn't want to risk contact with an armed girl who spends her days cutting up deaders so they can't get up again. I can't imagine what it must have looked like to a stranger to see me carefully severing the spines of deaders and then smashing their heads over and over before dragging them off to be pecked over by birds.

I shake my head and get back to the problem at hand. Namely, that I don't know where this address is and this is a big town. It isn't New York, but it isn't a little village either. Second, I have very little confidence in my driving ability, particularly through debris-strewn streets. I was learning to drive when all this happened, but I didn't even have my permit yet. Then again, my mom made sure there were arrangements for that contingency and I've continued according to her instructions. I just haven't actually practiced much open-road driving.

And as if I needed to add more to the pile, I have no idea how I'll corral five kids and then take care of them. And I don't know what to do about this Sam fellow, either. Those kids might think he's safe, but I don't have any past with him. There's no history of kindness and companionship between us to blind me to the menacing creature with snapping jaws he devolves into at the least little thing.

No, Sam is not safe to be around. I wish with all my might that I didn't know his name.

Trying to keep as low as I can in the grass, I make my way back to the sign. I can hide behind it and say what needs saying, do what needs doing if it comes down to that.

Sam has gone still again, looking at the deaders with a blank look on his face and his hands slack at his sides. In-betweeners are rarely still, so even this is odd and outside the expected norms, if that's even the right word to use.

Once I'm behind the big sign and peering through the narrow gap between its frame and brick base, I call out, "Sam."

He jerks like I've poked him with a stick and swings back toward the fence, his attention on the truck I was behind before. He's got enough memory-making capability inside him to remember that, so he must have been strong when he died, very healthy. It's a shame. It feels creepy to think it, but even like he is now, he's sort of cute.

Of course, that might be just the untrustworthy opinion of a teenaged girl who's been alone for a year and enjoyed a grand total of one date before the world went to crap. But, yeah, creepy thoughts.

It takes him a moment, but he seems to have regained his focus. No gnashing teeth or hungry eyes. He grips the rails again as if fortifying himself, and says, "Zam. Ya."

"Do you remember where the children are? Where Veronica is?"

He jerks at that name, his face twisting into something like pain. Then he bounces on his knees again. I'm growing more certain that's his way of nodding yes.

"Is it far?" I ask, and then realize how difficult it will be for him to answer that question. I amend it, asking, "Did you walk from there today?"

He bounces again, but I can clearly see the confusion on his face. I don't think he really understands the question. Time and distance are fairly advanced concepts.

"Which way to Veronica, Sam?"

One fist leaves the fence and, with great effort, he extends his fingers. His arm moves until he's pointing in the direction he wants before he grunts, "Da."

It's no more than I expected really and not nearly enough. I was sort of hoping—okay, really hoping—that he would point the other direction. Back that way lies the rest of the industrial park and some businesses. I've traveled that direction and there are no houses, hotels, or anywhere else where people might congregate after the end of the world. There's a big animal hospital down there, the one I went to in search of medicine for my mom, but that's about it for interesting destinations.

The direction he indicated leads into the city and the suburbs beyond. Basically, *everything* lies in that direction. Which doesn't narrow things down for me much. But, if I really think about it, he knew I was here, which means wherever he's from—wherever those kids still are—probably isn't too far away. I guess it's possible he came here because he was aware of the trucking hub and food distribution warehouse, and so has traveled some great distance, but I can't imagine many people knowing about this place. If that were the case, I would have been overrun at some point, and I haven't.

"Could we get back there today?" I ask him, not hoping for much because, you know, time is hard.

Sam shakes his legs in a sort of half-bounce, half-shuffle that is neither a yes or a no but says, "Ya. Kahm."

I may be a little too eager for company, but I've not lost all my senses. I can't just run off and follow an in-betweener who could turn on me at any time. He has bloodstains on him and those aren't from his wound. That means he's been eating. Maybe those kids are feeding him birds or something, but I don't know that and I doubt he'll be able to communicate that in a way I'd believe anyway. So, no, that's not going to happen right now.

"Are they safe? In a building? With food and water?"

"Ya," he answers. "Pardnad." Then his face twists again and I can see an agony of some deep sort in that twisted expression.

What a *pardnad* is I have no idea, so I think about his other words, the way he puts them together. Clearly, he meant that word to describe the situation the kids are in or the place they're at. That narrows it down some, but not enough.

"Is that where they are? Pardnad?" I ask.

He bangs his head against the rails of the fence again. The movement is so sudden and sharp that I almost stand, which would be a mistake. He grips the fence hard, his bloody and dirt-encrusted fingers paling with the force of it, and says, "Ah-pard-nad." He draws the word out, clearly trying to make it as intelligible as possible. It's amazing to me that a three-minutes-dead person can get out that much. But it works, because I understand him.

"They're in an apartment!" I call out.

He bounces, seeming to want me to go on. And I do want more information. An apartment rules out most of the suburbs, except perhaps at their edges. Downtown and the older parts of town are covered with them. And, of course, near the university there are endless blocks of them.

"Apartment complex or just a building?" I'm not sure he'll be able to get that one, so I try something different and say,

71

"Wait. I'm going to say some things. You let me know when I'm right. Okay?"

He bobs and says, "Ya."

For a second, just before his face moves back into that strange expression that flits between fear, hunger, anger, and combinations of those too complex to really understand, I think I see him smile. It's weird and crooked, but I think that's what it was and for some reason, it makes me feel good. Humans were simply meant to be smiled at, I think. Without the smiles of others, we lose our idea of what happiness looks like.

"Apartment complex. Lots of buildings," I offer. He stands still, or rather, as still as he can.

"One building."

At that, he bobs his knees and says, "Ya!"

That's actually not good. That means it isn't in some out-of-the-way place where there are few roads in or out. It might mean downtown.

"Downtown," I say, almost crossing my fingers in hope that he stands still. He does, but he's twitchier, like that was too vague or not quite right, but close. There's another possibility.

"College area?"

He bobs again and almost screeches, "Ya!"

"Are there other people around there?"

That question seems to bother him for some reason and he hangs his head, his fists working around the rails. But he doesn't bounce.

"No more people are there. Only people like you?" I ask. It's unlikely he calls in-betweeners by the same name that I do. It wasn't like I had anyone aside from my mother to share terminology with.

He bobs at that one, but more slowly, his head still hanging.

"And more like the ones at the gate?"

His bobbing continues, but he looks up and I see no smiles now, only anger and sadness. Overwhelming sadness.

That's another thing about in-betweeners. I've not had the chance to see many expressions on their faces other than needy hunger or blind rage, but their expressions are somehow more raw, unfiltered by social contract or fear of embarrassment. This must have been what humans were like long before we developed civilization.

Now, seeing all these emotions cross Sam's face with such absolute purity makes me understand how it was that humans first came together. If this is how we were with each other, then hiding our feelings and intentions would have been impossible. Honesty would have been the default mode for human interactions.

I've been alone too long and these mental tangents are not productive. My mind is turning a million miles a second, so fast it's almost nauseating. Just thinking about any one of the several options I'm considering is enough to make me want to hurl. Put all of it together, with no long-considered plan and no one to watch my back except an in-betweener who is really my biggest threat, and it's too much for my system.

I'm a person of careful habits and that is why I'm still breathing and thinking instead of like Sam. I'm about to toss that entire box of habits aside with both hands.

Before I can think too much more about it and regain my senses, I call out, "I can go tomorrow. I have to find a map, arrange transportation. I'm not just going to walk out there with you."

At the sound of my voice, I'm pretty sure he's going to go all in-betweener on me, but he doesn't. Instead, he jams his hands through the rails of the fence and puts his wrists together in the unmistakable sign for being handcuffed or tied. Then he presses his face to the bars, reminding me of a horror movie I once saw, and says, "Mehg sday."

I know what that means without asking. He knows he can't be trusted not to wander. He wants me to tie him to the rails of the fence and make him stay. His face makes me want to cry.

Three Years Ago - Mix and Match

My mother is worried. She won't tell me that, but I know she is. The way she tugs at her lips with her teeth and looks at me with those greedy, never-leave-me eyes, tells me she's girding herself for another frightening fight for my life.

I've been getting headaches again and, even though it should be a simple matter of getting another scan and verifying that it's just a headache and not my cancer returning, there are steps that must be followed.

Nanite treatment is no guarantee against a cancer coming back, at least not in my case. Newer nanites for first aid, infection reduction, or even plaque control continue working, replacing themselves and maintaining a healthy population number inside their host. These new ones are replicated within the host by specialized factory nanites.

Mine were the first of their kind, really, and it makes no sense to keep a bunch of machines in your head after the cancer is gone. So all of these new and more complicated nanites didn't exist during my treatment and that left my body to its own devices once my cancer was cured. But, like the doctor said, even one cancer cell left in my head has the chance to start the whole process over again. Probably not, but it *is* possible.

Yet, the headaches. My doctor has scheduled the scan, but he's told us that the more likely explanation is the growth of my skull around the scarred parts and my brain filling the space once taken up by cancer as I grow. That makes sense to me because I'm in a growth spurt the likes of which I never expected. The doctor says that's just because my body had a few years of falling behind, with messed-up hormones and all of that. I'm getting tall. I like tall.

I could also be in denial. It's an option.

Besides, I hate to say it, but if it is my cancer again, it's not like they don't know how to treat it. And they can do it better and with less pain than when I had it done the first time. They don't even drill into a patient's head anymore. For my second treatment, the nanites were simply shot into my spinal fluid and they did their thing. It's almost an out-patient procedure nowadays. Okay, maybe that's an exaggeration, but not a huge exaggeration.

"What's going on?" I ask, as our car nears the military hospital. The access road ahead is blocked and police vehicles crowd the intersection that leads off to the military shopping complex and gas station. Beyond a row of blockades, a crowd fills the road for as far as I can see.

My mother sits up higher in the seat, as if that added inch of height will somehow let her understand what's going on. "I don't know. I mean, I knew there were some demonstrations planned, but I didn't realize it was going to be here. Or like this!"

I check the clock on the car's dash and say, "I've only got an hour before my scan, Mom."

This is important information. These machines are in high demand, now more than ever, and I don't want to wait another week or two for another slot. I don't want my mom to have to wait another week or two.

A cop at the roadblock gestures with a bored wave of his hand for my mom to turn right, but she stops and lowers the window instead. The cop almost rolls his eyes as he takes a couple of steps forward at my mom's polite, "Excuse me, officer."

"Ma'am, you need to turn right. No, I won't let you go past. The road is blocked."

"Of course, officer," my mother says, the level of politeness undiminished as if she didn't hear the rudeness in his words. "I only want to ask where patients at the hospital are supposed to go. My daughter is a patient."

He leans down, eyes me, and asks, "Can she walk?"

I nod and say, "Sure."

"Then the officer at the end of the block will let you into the parking lot. If she can't walk that far, ask him for a chair and an attendant will come get her." He seems to realize then that we aren't the people turning his day into a pain in the butt, so he adds, "Sorry about this, ma'am."

A horn blares behind us and the cop steps back, leveling a look at the car that is anything but amused. He waves us to the right again.

There are cops everywhere. And where there aren't cops, there are security guards that look almost just like cops. No military cops, though. I'm guessing that wouldn't look good on the news. The guards all have the same wary looks, the same slightly angry stances. They do let us into the main hospital lot, which stretches like a discount store lot for forever, and I wonder how people who are physically restricted in some way manage to get to the doors. The front has patient drop-off, which is clearly not an option.

It's hot out and I'm sweating by the time we reach the doors. There are hospital security guards there as well, this time in military uniforms, and we're not even allowed inside the lobby until my mom shows her ID and my appointment is confirmed. Ironically, we're early.

We grab cold drinks from the machine in the lobby and then give each other a look that needs no explanation. We both want to know what's going on. Of course we do.

Near the front of the hospital the mood is tense, but through the glass I can see the crowds covering the front parking lot and spilling out into the street. Signs pepper the crowd with slogans like, "*Dead is Dead*" and "*Taxes Shouldn't Pay for Eternal Vegetables*" and even less flattering things. My favorite is the one that says, "*Keep Your Nanite Cooties to Yourself!*"

"Ah," my mother says at almost the same time I do.

This is the only nanite-certified hospital in a hundred miles, so it's the obvious focus for an anti-nanite demonstration, but I thought there were laws against interfering with access to places like this. And this is a military hospital right next to a military base, which should mean that this place is doubly protected from protests like this. Maybe the back lobby is considered access enough and maybe just being off the base itself is sufficient to make it open season for protests.

My mother worries at her lip again, then reaches absently for me, pulling me to her with an arm around my shoulder. Her hand brushes at my hair, perhaps unconsciously messing with my scar the same way I do.

"No one is going to stop giving nanites. If it has come back, I'll get my cure," I say quietly and lean my head on her shoulder.

She nuzzles my head and I can feel her cheek rise in a smile. "I know, baby. I know."

There's a delay with my appointment, but it's only a few minutes. The harried nurse escorts me into the changing area and gets me ready to go so that they can regain a few minutes of their screwed-up schedule. As a result, I'm stuck standing in the antechamber with an attendant and my IV hanging out of my arm. It's awkward, but it's also an ideal time for me to pump him for some information.

"What do you think is going to happen? Because of what's going on outside, I mean."

He shrugs. "Something's got to give. Every nursing home in fifty miles is full and people who shouldn't be sent home have to go home to families who can't properly take care of them," he says. His attitude is sort of uninterested, his voice a bit dismissive as if this were all old news. Maybe it is.

I'll readily admit that for the first year after my procedure, I was fascinated with everything nanite. I owe the nanites my life, the vision in my eye—however imperfect that might be—and every single experience I've had since the doctors put those little buggers into my head.

For another year after that, I was still interested, but no longer obsessed. The discoveries came too quickly for excitement to build and maintain itself. After another year of following the news only in the most casual way, I didn't just lose interest, I began to avoid the topic completely. I no longer wanted to be the girl whose brain was nearly eaten by cancer, but was saved by nanites. My mom seemed to recognize that and it quietly became a topic we avoided, one that made us change the channel on TV.

So, I basically have no idea what he's talking about.

"I'm sorry, I don't understand."

The attendant turns to me, arms crossed up high as if he's cold, and asks, "Really?"

I shake my head and try hard to look apologetic for my ignorance. But that appears to be unnecessary. It almost seems to excite him, like I'm a fresh new canvas he can paint bad news onto.

"All the deadheads. How are we supposed to take care of so many vegetables for ten, twenty…hell, *fifty* years? Think about it. We give nanites to these people whose hearts have stopped for whatever reason and it restarts their pumps most of the time, but what is really left? You can't just tell someone that it's been too long and you're not going to administer the nanites to their loved one. It's standard procedure for the

EMTs." He pauses, taps his head with a finger, and says, "No oxygen to the brain. Vegetables. If we're lucky they're brain dead and the family agrees to shut them down. Most of the time we're not that lucky."

"Ah," I say because I can't think of anything else to say. I get a picture in my mind of endless rows of perfectly healthy people who will never wake up again. I mean, half the people in this hospital probably have half a dozen different types of nanites running around inside their bodies. Who knows what that will do in the long run? You can buy some communist country's cheap-o versions on the internet now if you don't mind the possibility of getting caught by the postal inspector.

Before I can think of anything intelligent to say, he goes on. "I mean, look at it this way. Everyone dies. That's the price of living. We should play the hand we're dealt." He shoots a knowing look my way from under his lowered brow and adds, "We'll pay for screwing around like this. One way or another."

His last words hit me like a punch in the gut. He has no way of knowing that I'm one of those people who didn't play the hand she was dealt. There's no way he can know that he's telling me that I should have let myself die, that my mother should have let her only child die.

While my instinct is to say something mean, to cut him with some clever bit of sarcasm I can't think of just yet, I decide that I should forget it instead. I decide to forgive him for his inadvertent wish for my death. But I clamp my lips together to keep from saying something nasty in case my high-minded ideals leave me.

There's no need, though, because the door opens and another woman shuffles past, her hands pulling her robe tightly to her body and her eyes downcast. Hospital etiquette. I know these rules and I keep my eyes away from her as well. Preserving dignity is big in the chronic patient culture.

Now, it's my turn in the machine.

Today - Choices, Choices

I've never been this close to an in-betweener that I haven't filled full of bolts or arrows first. I don't have handcuffs or anything like that, but I do have zip ties. I keep a few in the front pocket of my backpack along with other necessities. They're handy for hanging larger things off my pack, like the handles of the jumbo bottles of stuff they have in that warehouse. It leaves more room in my pack. I'm an expert at reusing zip ties. I doubt very much anyone is making new ones, so I really hate wasting them.

I use the newest zip ties I have in my pack, the ones I figure probably still have the tightest lock on their little teeth. Sam loses it when he first sees me, of course, but he actually does manage to get himself under control. He holds his hands out again, palms pressed together like he's praying, and looks down. It's a quick procedure and the *zzzt* of the tie securing his hands makes me feel better.

I don't look at him or say anything more. I just turn and walk rapidly away. Running seemed to get him going before, so I'm going for something calmer and less provocative. It's such a long walk, but when I get behind the first building—an assembly building for perfumed sachets that still fills the air inside with a strong floral scent—I let my breath out in a relieved sigh.

Maps aren't something people used too much by the time all this went down, but I do know where one is. It's old, but even an old map has got to be better than nothing. Sticking to the visual shelter of the buildings, I make my way to my original destination this morning—the trucking hub for nonperishable groceries.

Inside, it's dark because I've shut all the big bay doors and stuffed plastic in the cracks to keep out as many vermin as I can. Even with that precaution, bags of rice and the like started developing little gnawed holes and food began to scatter soon after we got here. I emptied as much as possible into a bunch of barrels and plastic bins I collected from other buildings, but I've probably lost as much as I've kept. The concrete floor makes little crunching noises under my feet as I cross the vast space. These noises seem louder than normal today. The dirt and grit is building up faster than I can get rid of it. I take that as a sign that I need more people here. Even kids.

The office is old-fashioned and very well used, just as you'd expect a busy trucking office to be. Keeping it updated probably fell somewhere behind wallpapering their trucks in priority, I'm guessing. On the wall over a battered metal desk in the corner is a very old map with a trucking logo prominently displayed in the corner. It looks like something that should have a pin-up-girl calendar right above it, it's so old.

It's not much, but it's all I have. I've been through the trucks before, and don't remember any local maps in any of them. I would have grabbed anything as useful as a map when I scooped up all the pulp-fiction novels I found inside the cabs. I'd have done it just to have more to read, if nothing else. My mother had a map, but we lost it along with the extra backpacks—and extra weight—during our escape from the law offices.

I pull out the paper with the address and shine my flashlight onto the tiny print covering the bottom third of the map. Streets are listed in alphabetical order. If this place is near the college, then even if the building is new, the street would have been there for ages.

And there it is. The coordinates listed—alphabetical along the bottom and numerical along the side—show the street smack-dab in the middle of the college area of town, which is to say, old downtown. It's a place of narrow streets, curbside parking, and very poor sight lines. In short, it's possibly the worst place I might venture into and still hope to remain in one piece.

But, on the upside, the deaders are truly dying—or slowing way down—and the in-betweeners are becoming deaders much faster due to lack of living food. While I would expect that area to be a crowded mess, it's possible that they've died off there even faster than out here. I mean, what's left to eat once all the apartment cats and Chihuahuas are gone?

My positive outlook subsides as my finger traces a path on the map back to where we are now, on the outskirts past the entire downtown area. I'll either have to go through that part of town, or take a long and circuitous route around it. That will invite anyone who might have survived out where the sight lines improve to grab themselves one teenaged girl.

I have two real options. Well, two options aside from the obviously saner choice of just forgetting the whole thing. I could find a way to secure Sam and go on foot, hoping he'll keep other in-betweeners away from me should there be any. I don't know if that actually provides any protection, but the in-betweeners seem to have a sense for a fresh host, much the same way the deaders do, and I've not seen them attacking each other very much. It does happen, of course. If two in-betweeners want the same meal, some very aggressive encounters can ensue. But they're more like animals when that happens. It's all very primitive. Otherwise, they tend to avoid each other, almost like they have a sense for territory and know when a territory is claimed.

My other option feels like the safer one in my gut, but perhaps not safer where other humans are involved. I have a vehicle and I have the means to charge it. It will take a while, but my mother taught me how to maintain the two systems and I have done so religiously. The vehicle is electric and quiet, but it would be a moving vehicle in a world without them. There's no way a human could miss that if I entered their range of view. Nothing in nature moves as fast as a car, so it will stand out like a blimp.

And then there are the conditions of the roads to consider. And…and…and. The list of considerations is endless. So, I'll do what my mom taught me to do. I'll make a list and then work the list. I fear it will be a long list.

Two Years Ago -
Miscommunications

My mother rushes into our house, barking orders as she does. "Emily, don't ask questions. Just go pack. Your camping gear, not your normal clothes. Put on your hiking boots and sturdy clothes. *Do it!*"

The door slams behind her with so much force that the glass in the sidelights rattles, creating shivers in the rainbows projected onto the floor by the angled glass. She tosses her bag down, the computer inside making a fatal-sounding *thunk* against the baseboards.

She doesn't even flinch at the sound, which more than her words tells me she's serious. That computer is her life. When she finally retired from the military, she eagerly took a job doing computer programming with the same biotech firm that created my nanites. She's dedicated. She says no mother should lose a child and that's a strong motivator for her. She's been on a long shift—four days in fact—because of some new project, so I haven't seen her since she left.

I stand there looking at the computer for a second too long and she barks, *"Go!"*

She never yells at me. Maybe she did when I was really little, before I got sick, but I don't remember much of my early years, so I have no way of knowing. A side effect of having your brain squished for a long time is a somewhat fragmented memory, I guess. But since then, no, she never yells.

And she just did.

I startle at the sharp tone, the new fear blossoming inside me made worse because I have no idea why she's so afraid. But her harsh voice works, because I rush to do as she says.

In my room, I call for the TV to show me the news. I have an "emotional intensity" block on the news so I haven't watched any news at all in almost a year. It's all just terrorists and diseases and it freaks me out. I prefer avoidance. It's an excellent strategy most of the time.

As I pack, I remove the block and see for the first time what's been brewing in the world outside. It's summer break, so I haven't gone beyond the little pool in our backyard in at least a week. Okay, maybe it's been two weeks. Don't judge me. I'm enjoying the break from school and having zero obligations, so I've missed all of it while I wallow in my haze of chlorinated water, sunshine, and potato chips. What I see makes me stop in my tracks, my camping pack hanging empty in my hands.

It looks like people are having a riot, only one in which biting is the preferred method of attack. And many of them appear to be wearing hospital gowns, their butts in plain view, a situation they don't seem to mind at all. Some are even naked. But not all of them. It's hard to tell who is rioting and who is running from the riots. Even some of the cops seem to be getting in on the fighting on the wrong side. And everywhere I look on the screen there are splashes of red. On the people, on the pavement, on the cars, everywhere there is the gleaming red of spilled blood.

"Emily! Pack!" my mother yells from her room. I hear the sounds of drawers slamming and a closet door banging as it reaches the limits of its sliding rails.

I shake out of my TV trance, open my backpack, and do as my mother said. By the time I have my pack put together, I realize how light it is, how light it will be compared to hers. That's how we've had to be before, but since my second round of nanites, I'm clear of cancer once again. And I'm stronger than ever before.

I take my pack, with its loads of extra space and light contents, to my mother's room. It looks like she's tossed the room, like she's burgling our home.

"Mom, I can take more than this," I say, holding out the big framed pack.

She bites at her lip, eyes the pack and then me. She says, "Honey, I don't want you doing more than you can." Then she shakes her head and corrects herself. "No, forget that. I don't want you loaded down with more than you can carry and still run. Go get all the freeze-dried meals and pack those. Get some water bottles—not too many—and pack those. That's enough."

I turn to leave, then stop and say, "Mom, I'm scared. Please just tell me what's going on. I'll do what you say, but please."

My voice sounds shivery, like I'm suddenly a scared nine-year-old again, and I hate it. I've been scared a lot in my life, so I thought I'd become a braver person than this. But my mom is not the kind of person who acts like she has been for the past twenty minutes, and that is shaking the foundation I've built my world upon. Her strength is mine and this woman with her jerky movements and wide, nervous eyes is messing with my ability to deal with it.

She sighs and, for a moment, lowers her head over the pack that she's been stuffing full. Then she takes in a deep breath and walks over to me. I can tell she's trying to slow down, to pretend that she's not in a frantic rush, but her too-hard steps and strained face give her away. She strokes my head, pushing my hair back and away from my face, and gives me a shaky smile.

"Sweetie, I don't have time to explain everything, but something has gone wrong with the broadcast."

I have no idea what she's talking about, and she sees it in my face, because she cups her hand around the side of my head and says, "The nanite update broadcast."

"So," I say, still not understanding.

"I heard your TV on. You saw?" she asks.

I nod, thinking of the hospital-gowned people. "It's making people riot? Protesters?"

"Emily, they aren't rioting and those aren't protesters. Those are patients and they've been updated. Or, at least some of them are patients. It's gone beyond them already. It didn't work." Her hand drops from my head and she lets out a sudden laugh, but not one of humor. "That's an understatement."

I shake my head, not at all clear about what she's saying. She's been excited for a few weeks about a new project at work, but she's almost always excited so I haven't paid much attention. All I know is that they are working on a way to enhance neural activity for people who were left unable to wake up after administration of emergency nanites.

"We don't have a lot of time here, Emily. The short version is that this update was supposed to help those who were infused with First Responders after too long without oxygen to the brain. That's why they are like they are—brain-damage. This was supposed to help that by updating the internal nanite factories to shift production to a form of neural-correction nanite. And allow the First Responders to maintain oxygen levels for longer by stimulating circulation."

"I saw...I saw them biting, I think," I offer, hoping for something more complete in terms of explanation.

"Emily, you understand about the layers of the brain, about the primitive versus the modern," she says. It's not a question.

"Yeah. I know a lot about the brain. You know that," I answer.

My mother's eyes dart to the window as the faint sound of a shot travels through. When she looks back at me, her expression is one I can't really translate. It's like every bad emotion a person can have flies across, one after the other. Most of all, I see fear.

"When we updated them, what we woke up was the oldest part of the brain. The part that knows to eat, to run, to fight. It knows nothing else."

I look away from her and think. If a person is so damaged that they can't wake up, but then is forced in some way to wake up without access to those higher thought centers that make us human, what are they? Another series of shots sounds out in the distance and I see my mom's shoulders tighten.

"Like animals?" I ask her.

"Worse, but that's a good enough description for now," she says. I can tell she's listening for more noises outside in our suburb.

"Will they get better?" I ask.

My mom grimaces and returns her attention to the backpack, at least superficially. Her jaw clenches and she stuffs two boxes of ammunition into the side pockets of her pack. The gun case is sitting on the bed, the black plastic looking ominous atop the bright floral pattern of her comforter. Her military boots are on the bed, a revival of her recent past.

She zips the pocket closed with a hard motion. I see her fix her gaze on the gun case. She doesn't look up at me when she says, "Just be glad your nanites are gone."

Her voice is so dead flat when she says it that I shiver. After that, I hurry.

Today - Blue Slushies

Usually, I try not to look at the car more than I have to. When I come to do maintenance on it, I sort of let my eyes slide over the things that made it ours. The little dent where I hit it with my bike, the stain on the driver's seat where my mom dropped an entire blue slushie into her lap, the stickers on the back of her and me in cartoonishly simple outlines.

No, I don't like to look at those things anymore. They bring memories. The way she squealed when the icy mass hit her lap and how she bounced around until we pulled over. The way we laughed when she got out, shedding chunks of blue ice into the gutter as she danced around.

I'm surprised to find that I'm smiling as that memory surfaces. That's a first.

I can't remember a single time in the past year when I've thought of something like that from a more normal time and not cried. I like this new feeling. It's not happy so much as not completely sad. It's a mixture of missing her, loving her, being sad that she's gone, and being grateful for that day. It's good. I think that's how it's supposed to be.

I really, really hope I get more chances to feel that way.

With that sobering thought, I'm suddenly cognizant of everything I still need to do. I'm burning daylight and will need to be on the road as soon as first light. And I'd sure like to get some sleep so I can be at my most aware when I do leave.

Since I don't have to worry about gassing anyone to death with the fumes, I set up the little emergency generator in the office furniture warehouse where I keep the car. It's not a regular generator, but one meant just for our car. It even has a matching paint job, the same silvery-blue as the car. Except the car's paint is pretty faded now. My mom liked to be prepared for anything and given her love of camping, this thing was a must. It was sort of a big joke between us that we had to pack a gas can when camping just for our electric car.

I've been driving the car around the complex just enough to keep the tires supple and the batteries in good working order. I use it to listen for radio transmissions, but there are never any to hear, just endless dead air. I pipe my music-player songs through it very quietly once in a while, but I can usually only handle a song or two before it gets depressing. I can't help but wonder if whoever sang each song is dead or staggering around gnawing on metal. That train of thought generally makes it a lot harder to enjoy the music.

The car doesn't let me down. The charge is still good, holding fine and only in need of a top-off. I leave the generator to do its job and go get the next thing on my list.

One of the cars in the lot where employees parked has one of those dog fences installed between the front and back seats. I'd made a note of it before, but since I didn't need it at the time, I'd left it in place. The doors are locked and that means busting out a window. I prefer not to do things like that unless and until I really need to. And now I do. It's not the same kind of car as ours, but I'm pretty sure the fence adjusts to different kinds of cars.

It turns out there's a great deal of swearing involved in installing one of those fences. Without instructions, that is especially true. But in the end, I feel it's in there so tight that one more turn on the bolts would make them poke right through the floorboard of the car.

I'm less comfortable with the gap around the center where a hump should be. And the proximity of those little open squares of space framed by the thick wires is just plain disturbing. When I poke my fingers through the holes and push as hard as I can, all I do is make my hand hurt, so I think it's secure.

Sam has shown himself to be cut from slightly different cloth than the other in-betweeners though, so I make sure there's nothing at all in the back that he could use to poke at me through the holes. I even check down in the gaps between seats when I fold them down to make a bigger holding area for him. There are no tools, but I do find a wild assortment of ancient candy wrappers and french fries. I don't know what else I might expect from him, so I'm treating this entire situation as if he's got all the marbles of a regular human.

I might have mentioned it before, but caution and carefulness are the most valuable habits a person can have today. It might even be true that the only people who are alive today are those that have those habits deeply engrained. So yes, I'm tossing out petrified fast food particles and wrappers along with the bobby pins and broken pencil I find deep between the seats.

As much as I'd like to focus on the car for the rest of the day, there's more to do and I'm not looking forward to this next part at all. The birds are everywhere and they especially seem to like it here in my little complex. While it might be the flat roofed buildings or the lack of deaders and in-betweeners nearby, I like to flatter myself it's because they like my company.

Whatever the reason, there are hundreds of them on the rooftops around me. I do take some for food, but not on the roof. I don't want to give them any reasons to relocate. I'd be too lonely without them.

Instead, I take those whose flights cross my path. That way I can at least partially delude myself that they might not live here. Unfortunately, I can't settle for any maybes tonight. I need birds and a lot of them. I grab my crossbow and my bundle of bolts that have lines attached to them, then step out into the big open area in the center of my circle of warehouses.

At least fifty pairs of eyes inspect me from the rooftops when I close the door behind me. Mostly pigeons and doves, they all bristle with attitude and frank curiosity about the human in their midst. I crack a smile because I can't help it, but then it falls away when I think about what I have to do.

I just hope they don't leave because of what I'm about to do. And I'm doing it for a captive in-betweener, which makes me question myself even more. How is this a good idea?

Whatever. I've got to do it. Giving my shoulders a roll to loosen up the muscles, I put the first bolt in and then lift it, aiming for a daring pigeon eyeing me with its head cocked to the side and not a bit of suspicion. "I'm sorry," I whisper and let the bolt go.

*****

By the time I'm satisfied with my preparations, I'm starving *and* a bundle of nerves, which makes it hard to actually get down to the process of eating. Instead, I push around the rice in my bowl and stare at it. I stupidly covered the bland rice with some canned tomatoes. The gloopy red color reminds me too much of blood. It reminds me of what I just got done doing and what might happen to me tomorrow. Eventually, I close my eyes and just shovel it in, fighting nausea and swallowing each bite only through force of will.

Once it gets full dark, which is surprisingly late in the summer—something I hadn't much noticed in my previous, artificially lighted existence—I spare the crankable lanterns and nestle down into my bed. I've made a bedroom out of one of the smaller offices up on the observation platform. The metal stairs will give me fair warning of approach and the room is small enough that it never gets ridiculously cold in the winter. Body heat is surprisingly effective when you have a good sleeping bag, an air mattress, and a small space.

This particular office has only a small window that's easy to cover with cardboard, so it's the only place I feel comfortable keeping lit after dark, but tonight, I just want to try to sleep and not think about the in-betweener outside. I've been keeping half an ear open for noises, but if he's making any, it's been quiet enough that it doesn't travel far on the still night air. If I could have done so, I would have gagged him, but there's no way I could risk getting that close to his mouth.

Sleep doesn't come easily, but it finally does. And with sleep come dreams of blue slushies and my mother, laughing.

Twenty Months Ago – The Lake of Dreams

I think we're going to have to leave here soon. Every time I bring it up, my mother waffles over the decision. One day she's certain we'll go, another that we'll stay. I understand how hard it is to decide that. I really do. It's not like we can be certain of safety anywhere else, and this place is what we're used to now.

The hunting isn't great today and I adjust my butt on the uncomfortable branch in the tree I'm stationed in. The cabin is no more than fifty yards away, but the trees are so thick that I can only see hints of it through the foliage blowing in the fall breeze. The rustling of all the leaves is almost too loud for me to hear anything over, but it also covers my noises as I fidget, so it's a trade-off.

My mother is in another tree about twenty yards away and I can see her feet where they hang down from the branch. They kick once in a while, so I know she's getting uncomfortable too. It's been a long morning.

A slightly louder and more purposeful rustling makes me peer into the shadows. Human or animal? Dead or alive?

In my ear, the walkie talkie comes to life with my mom's whispered voice. I press the earbud into my ear and hear her say, "Pig. Small. We can eat that."

I swallow hard at her words. So far, I've shot rabbits and squirrels, but nothing bigger. It took a lot to get over the idea of killing and eating an animal. I'm not one of those idiots who think no animals get hurt and that meat in the stores is born on white plastic foam trays, but the doing of that is a far different thing than just knowing that's how it happens.

A pig? A small pig that might even be cute?

Sucking in a deep—but quiet—breath, I press the chirp button on my radio twice, sending her the signal for "yes" without speaking. The rustling comes again, but this time accompanied by a little grunting noise, and from the shadows shuffles the pig in question. It's small, near black, and just as I feared, very cute.

"Dang-it," I breathe.

I'm still not entirely comfortable with the crossbow, but I'm so glad we have them. It's been fun learning it, just not so fun using it on things with heartbeats. The pig—more of a piglet really—is jumpy, looking around almost as soon as it begins nosing through the underbrush and old leaf litter. With good reason. There have been more and more of those crazy in-betweener people running around, even out here at the lake. They would go after a pig as fast as they would a human.

Maybe that's why this youngster is on its own. Not for long, though.

Sighting in the piglet, who has politely turned away a little so that I have a side shot, I silently apologize and pull the trigger. The whomp of the bolt letting go comes only a microsecond before the squeal.

*****

My mom is super-fast and I'm very grateful for that. It took two bolts and a short chase, but we got our piglet. We should wind up with more than twenty pounds of good meat. It was a lot bigger than it looked like from up a tree.

Unfortunately, we aren't the only ones to hear the piglet. An in-betweener shows up within moments, that angry shouting preceding it and giving us the warning and time we need to hustle back into the cabin and shut ourselves in with the dead pig.

After racing around the cabin to lower the wooden beams over the doors, we leave the pig in the kitchen sink and lock ourselves into the bathroom. The window there is boarded shut with metal over the outside and wood on the inside. It's as lightproof as we can make it. The other windows in the cabin are boarded up, but this room is the safest one in the place.

Quietly, I trickle water from a bucket over my mom's hands and she washes the blood off, letting it drain away in the bathtub. Her head is on a swivel, listening as the in-betweener makes progress around the cabin.

"He smells the blood," I whisper in her ear.

She nods, her lips tightly pressed together and her hands raw from scrubbing them. An impact on the wall nearby registers as a tremor in the cabin and we crouch on the floor, trying to stay still and wait until the in-betweener finds something else to focus on.

Eventually, the screams stop, but the in-betweener is still roaming around. As he comes close to the bathroom window, faint scratching sounds and grunts trickle in. After an hour or more, he screams again and takes off. I can tell he's going for the woods behind the cabin.

Both of us let out a pent up breath when he's gone and my mom ruffles my hair. "Good job," she says, as if I had done nothing more unusual than vacuuming the living room without being told. Our lives have changed so drastically and profoundly, I have no idea what's normal anymore.

"So," I begin, opening the bathroom door so we can get back to the business at hand, "do you know how to make bacon?"

My mother shakes her head and laughs quietly. "You have a one-track mind, you know."

I press against her as we walk and she puts her arm around my shoulder, brushing my head with her cheek in that way she does. It's a good feeling. We've got food, but not much in the way of meat and I've been craving it in the worst way. It's nice to know that I've helped put it on the table.

Grabbing her hand as we walk through the cabin, I say, "You didn't answer the question. Do you know how to make bacon?"

Squeezing my fingers, she chuckles. "No, but I can make a mean plate of spare ribs. Will that do?"

Oh yes, that will definitely do.

*****

The pig is gone and it's time to try to hunt again. It's getting harder to find animals. I remember this place as being filled with wildlife before, but now it's getting thinned out by the in-betweeners. The lake has fish in it, but going onto the lake means being in the open where anyone can see us. In-betweeners might not be able to swim, but what if some can?

And in-betweeners aren't the only things we have to worry about anymore.

Hearing gunshots isn't that unusual now, though the noise drawers more in-betweeners. Even so, if you're in a situation where it's either shoot or die, most people will shoot. Not too long ago, we heard a lot of shooting. At least fifty gunshots in total, but it was far away, further around the lake.

At the time, we thought it might be a group of in-betweeners. That happens sometimes. They scream when they sight food, which draws more of them. Sometimes they fight over the spoils, but most of the time they just eat and only get irritated with each other once they're done. If more food shows up, then you've got your in-betweener group already formed.

If that keeps going for a while, then you can wind up with a large group of them. Dozens strong, they're almost unstoppable at that point. Luckily, they also don't like to be in a group like that and the groups tend to dissipate on their own.

The day after we heard those gunshots, we investigated, though very quietly and using as much stealth as possible in case there were more in-betweeners. And yes, there were some there, but only a couple and those looked like they had been drawn by the noise rather than acting as the cause of it. No bloody bullet wounds, no holes in faces.

It was people that did it. It looked to us like someone raided a cabin and cleaned it out. They left behind six bodies. Humans.

So, yeah, fishing on the lake out in the open isn't our first choice anymore. Or our third.

Leaves are falling and the trees aren't going to be the best cover for us pretty soon. I'm not sure how we're going to survive the winter here, but my mom says we can. I have my doubts.

Usually, mom walks me to my tree and waits for me to get up safely before going off to her own, but today she merely watches me from a distance, not yet climbing her tree, but waiting at its base for me to get there and climb. I take it to mean she's gaining confidence in me. I like that.

At the base of my tree, I pause and look around, listening intently for anything amiss. I don't hear anything, but I immediately see something out of place. There's a backpack lying tilted at the base of a tree a little further into the forest. Since it's bright blue and still looks good, it can't have been here long. It's not like I would miss something like that.

A backpack means a person, or someone who was recently a person.

I back up, my fingers searching for the transmit button on the radio at my belt. My mom must see my alarm, because the circuit opens. "I'm coming," she half-whispers.

By the time I depress the button to answer, I feel her hand at my shoulder. She's got her crossbow up and is scanning the trees around me. I point toward the backpack and she takes her hand off the crossbow again for just long enough to tap me and point back toward the cabin.

We walk carefully, even more than usual, until the wooden walls of the cabin scrape against my back. My mother lets out a loud breath, her eyes still roaming as if she's trying to see in all directions at once. Then she brushes her hand down the side of my head and pulls me to her shoulder. I can hear her heart thundering in her chest, that hollow sound of her lungs as she breathes.

"Are you okay?" she asks in a whisper. "Did you see anything?"

I shake my head, not sure if I should be as scared as she is. It was just a pack.

Eventually, she shuffles us toward the door, her eyes still scanning and her arm tight around me. The crossbow is still up, but shaking a little, so she has to be getting tired. Once we're inside, she bolts the door and puts in the brace, then she goes to the "spotting holes" she has bored into each of the window coverings, pulling the plugs she has in them to hide our light at night. As she scopes out our surroundings, her fingers clench into fists, then loosen again.

"Why are you so scared, Mom?" I ask her.

She glances back, makes a little face at my choice of words, then says, "Why would someone put a filled pack right there in the open?"

I shrug, but say, "Because they were being chased and dropped it to go faster? Because it was on an in-betweener and it finally fell off? Because a million reasons."

My mom finishes with the final window then turns to me, a half-smile on her lips. "You're a smart girl, aren't you?"

Again I shrug, but I still smile. I love it when she says stuff like that when I can tell she really means it.

After sitting down, she pats the couch cushions next to her and I sit. Then I know she's going to be serious because she grips my knee and gives it a squeeze. "Emily, it could be those reasons, but I didn't hear anyone having a fight out there, did you? Or an in-betweener out back screaming?"

When I shake my head, she says, "That's a nice pack, clearly very full and with lots of great tools hanging off the sides in full view. Very tempting. It could easily be a trap. For all I know, someone who knows we're here—or that other cabins are occupied—could have left it just to put us into a firing line, or to distract us while they circled around to attack or something."

"Doesn't seem likely to me," I say.

She laughs. "Maybe not, but do you want to take that chance?"

"Nope," I answer, quite truthfully, then I add—also quite truthfully, "But I'd sure like to get a look inside that pack."

My mom laughs again.

Today – A Night Full of Terrors

I wake to the sound of screams. It's late, as in very late. I can tell simply by the way I feel. For a second, I think maybe I've dreamed the screams—which would be entirely natural given the situation—but then it comes again. I'm positive that it's Sam.

The problem is that those are not regular in-betweener screams at all. They're almost frightened, like he means for me to hear them. And I couldn't possibly miss them. He's very, very loud.

I scramble to my feet, sling my rifle over my back, and grab my crossbow. I don't have time to kit up, not with his screams rising in volume and sounding increasingly frantic. Jamming my feet into an old pair of Vans—no laces, so those are my go-to emergency shoes—I'm running for the door without even so much as a peek outside first. I've never, ever done that before. Sam has been here less than a day and he's already messed up my long-established routines.

At least I have enough of my wits to stop myself from bursting out of the side door without looking. Outside that small square of window, I can only see the back of the complex between the buildings and the open space that backs all the buildings. There's nothing out of place at all. My pots of tomato plants and the bushy squash plants inside half-barrels that sprang leaks are shivering in the nighttime breeze, but there's no other movement.

I can't see the birds on the roof in the deep dark, but now I hear them too. Disturbed squawks and coos rise and fall.

Something is here.

Sam lets out another scream, but this time I hear pain in it. Screw it. I push open the door and step out, looking everywhere at once. I'm good at it. Living now is like being in the middle of a battle that never ends, only pauses now and then so I can catch my breath before fighting again.

With no walls between us, I hear the added sounds of metal clanging and I know exactly which metal that is. It's my front fence, the specific tone created by impacts against the wrought iron unmistakable to my ears. Darting around the buildings, I decide against the road, since that's where Sam saw me go before. Instead, I'll go around the other side and use the trees planted around this complex to make it seem less industrial as cover.

It's dark out, the moon having set already, so all I have are the innumerable stars to see by. As bright as they are, it's not enough and everything is painted in shades of silver and black. It's only my familiarity with this place that lets me get around with little noise.

When I reach the corner of the building, I peek out through the cover of the dogwood trees toward the fence where I left Sam tied. I can't see much, but I do see movement. It's erratic and jerky, a flash of brighter silver where lighter colors move. And I think I see what the problem is right away.

While Sam is a mere dark smudge with a flash of light where his t-shirt shows, there's a blob of near white flailing around near him. He screams again, but this time, I hear a slightly higher-pitched and weaker scream with it. I think another in-betweener is there. Is it attacking Sam?

Switching my crossbow for my rifle, I try to see what's going on through the scope. Alas, all it does is magnify the darkness. I can't see. It's just too dark. I'll have to get closer if I want to do anything about this.

But should I?

"Bleeping hades," I mutter and dart between the trees. Of course, I'll do something about it. While I'm telling myself it's because an in-betweener having a tantrum will draw more in-betweeners here, I know there's a part of me that doesn't want Sam hurt. It's stupid and I can't explain it, but there it is.

Confirmation of my thought that there might be another in-betweener comes in the form of an extremely high-pitched scream. When I get within fifty feet of the fence, I hunker down behind the sign I hid behind just the day before with Sam. There's something wrong with the scream, the voice. It's not that it's garbled so much as sounding obstructed. There's a squealing sort of quality to it.

There's nothing wrong with Sam's voice though, other than the pain that makes it rise in pitch until the hair on my arms stands on end. I hear another clang as something impacts the fence.

At this point, my nerves are shot. I have to know what's going on. If this is an in-betweener climbing my fence, then I have to know it. It's happened before, though not very often. I keep my smells to a minimum outside the warehouses and the spikes on top of the fence often keep them in place for me to get a bead on as soon as they try to get over. But I can't afford to have one loose in here, especially not now when there is so much to do.

There's a very bright flashlight strapped to my rifle in just the position I need to light up a potential target. I don't use it often because it gives that same target something to focus on. Am I close enough for it to work? There's only one way to find out.

Clicking on the light, it sends a military grade beam of bright light directly toward the kerfuffle at the fence. What I see makes my heart sink into my shoes and my soul want to crawl into a hole, never again to see the light of day.

It's a child in-betweener. Those are the absolute worst. That explains the high pitch, but the wound on her neck explains the strange quality to her voice. How she died is very clear. She's wearing bright pink pajamas.

"No," I whisper. "Why?"

She flinches at the light, then flings herself back at the fence again. She's too small to climb it, but not at all fearful of throwing herself at it as if she might just barrel through it. Sam is kicking at her, his hands still secured by that great big zip tie I used. There is blood running down his side and seeping down his face. I don't think this child in-betweener was after me at all, but rather Sam.

Maybe his differences are as obvious to her as they are to me. What is he? An in-between in-betweener?

"Garah!" he yells. Well, he remembers me.

When he shouts, the little in-betweener throws herself at him, clamping down on his arm like a rabid dog, even shaking her head in that way dogs did when people played tug with them. She couldn't have been more than five years old when this happened to her. And she's still fairly new. Not as fresh as Sam, but not as aged as most of the others.

That makes me pull up short. That means there are more people near enough to me that a small in-betweener could make it here.

My mom and I had a policy about this sort of thing. Kids are the hardest to deal with. The temptation is to leave them. They are so small and they were children. But it's cruel to leave them like they are. Our policy was that we never left the child ones to roam.

Tears are falling down my face and my chest hurts like it's being squeezed in a vice as I sight her, the bluish light of my flashlight illuminating her in sharp detail. Her face is pretty even now, sweet and delicate. But she's not a child. She's a monster, no longer human in any way. I have to remember that. I pull the trigger while doing my best not to think about doing it.

Her head jerks like I hit it with a hammer and she flies away from Sam, who jerks and wails at his spot on the fence. He stops short and stares at her as she begins to jerk around on the ground, her tiny heels banging on the street's surface in a way that should have been painful. Now that I see them, the bottoms of her feet are shredded, the skin worn nearly away and that strange nanite scar tissue evident as it healed the continued abuse her feet took.

I feel for her, but I also can't let her get back up again.

The deaders at the fence are all wandering about at the ruckus and when I shine my light around, I see more of them shuffling across the street from wherever they were before. Not good. I can't go out there and smash up her head, so I've got to take care of the problem at a distance. I'm probably going to lose a lot of bolts doing this and I really, really hate that.

I'll hate it even more when I retrieve them.

Sam is still making strange sounds, a cross between a grunt and a scream, his eyes riveted to the bucking one-time child. That's now the loudest noise and I have to stop him. Leaving the safer shelter of the sign, I run for the fence. I have to do this from closer in, so I'll need to risk being near Sam and just hope that he settles down once the deed is done and I leave the area.

I just hope his zip ties hold. I've never tested them to this extent. If they break, then I might have to switch my aim to him and I don't want to. My plans have been formulating as I worked last evening and I'm going to need him, I think.

When he sees me, his head drops and he growls, ratcheting up for a good old yell.

"Sam! Be still! Be quiet!" I hiss at him as I get within range. He doesn't seem to hear me, his face full-on feral at this point. Ripping the velcro holding my light to my rifle, I flip it around my back and swing the crossbow back to the front. He watches me, his teeth clacking together so loudly it makes me flinch.

"Remember the kids, Sam. The kids need help!" I say to him, trying to get him to remember and lose his growing focus on me as prey.

That seems to work, because he glances back over at the bucking child and whines a terrible, pained whine. The emotional agony inside that sound is unmistakable. I shove my pity aside and aim my light and crossbow at the girl. I'm not going to get great shots with her moving like that. Right now I'm counting on speed and volume for effectiveness.

The bolts fly and most make contact, but when she finally stops moving, her head looks like a pincushion and I feel like I'm going to puke my guts out. Doing this is necessary, I know that, but that doesn't really make it easier. It takes out chunks of my spirit that can never be returned to me, even when I know it's the right thing to do.

Sam is looking at the girl now and when I shift my light to him, he barely flinches at the brightness. The expression on his face is one I'll never forget. It is grief and horror, sadness of a magnitude even I have difficulty comprehending and I've had plenty of reasons to feel some serious sadness.

He turns toward the light, his eyes narrowing against the bright beam, but there's no more feral hunger there. That has passed. He seems almost human. Well, human except for the oozing bite wounds all over him where the girl in-betweener went after him.

"Garah," he says, as if confirming to himself that it's me.

"I'm here," I whisper back.

Beyond the light, I hear the sliding, whispering noises of deaders still disturbed by the ruckus as they shuffle around. What I don't hear are any more in-betweener calls, like I would if there were more coming, alerted to food by the child in-betweener or Sam. I let out a breath after another minute of listening, relief bowing my shoulders and making me feel like I've just tried to lift a mountain. Fear is tiring.

Sam is still looking my direction, so I turn off the light and plunge us both into darkness. For him, the darkness should be more complete since the light was in his eyes. I take that opportunity to creep through the tall grass as quietly as I can.

From behind me, I hear one more soft and agonized, "Garah," before I get out of range. As the warehouse door closes softly behind me, the puking finally starts. I have no idea how long I sit there heaving, but with each heave I see that girl's face.

I hate this life.

Nineteen Months Ago – Stonerville

The pack belonged to a guy now encamped in the stoner's house. My mom doesn't like that I call them that. She says they are respected businessmen who fill a valid need in society. I don't care what she says, they're potheads. Before the end of the world, I used to watch them from the community dock when I swam on the lake. They were always out on their porch or on their private dock, passing a joint between them.

Personally, I don't know how they made any money given their love of their product.

Still, they own—owned?—one of the nicest cabins on this part of the lake. It's really more a house than a cabin. It's super nice and even has a roof deck. I've always envied them that roof deck.

The stoners are dead, or rather, one is dead and the other is dead-ish. He's an in-betweener and he's been roaming the woods around here for over two months now. My mom hasn't been able to get him with more than one decent shot, so he's still around. Or maybe he is. I haven't seen him in a few weeks, so maybe someone else got him by now.

I've got one of mom's peepholes open so I can see down the incline toward the lake—and the stoner house. The guy that's living there now is on the little dock that goes with that house. He's got a fishing pole in the water and his head on a swivel. He's never going to catch a fish if he keeps jerking around like that.

"Are you sure he doesn't know we're here?" I ask my mom. She's got one of the boards off the windows at the back of the house as she installs hinges at the top of it. She already did the one on the outside of the glass—it's sort of a plywood sandwich—and I think having it off for so long is making her more nervous than usual.

We don't use the fireplace here because of the smoke, but we have a camp-stove that we use for cooking and she's getting worried about the lack of air flow. We can't leave the plywood off, so hinges are a nice solution. That way we can open them to air out the cabin and secure it again quickly. Alas, we have no drill, so she's struggling to get the screws in manually. We got the hinges from the cabinets, so now we have no cabinet doors. It looks weird.

She shakes the fatigue out of her hand then bends back to the screwdriver. "I don't know for sure, but I don't think so. I would have expected him to be more curious if he did."

"Maybe that's why he didn't search our cabin when he started going through the others," I suggest.

That makes her stop and put down the screwdriver, using one hand to massage the soreness out of the other. She shrugs a little and says, "Maybe. But it might just be the blood and how close we are to the trees up here at the edges."

I only grunt at that. My mom is far more sneaky and sly than I ever realized. She came out of the woods one day after we killed an in-betweener that got caught in one of her wire traps spread between the trees. She was carrying a bucket and inside that bucket was blood. Then she proceeded to creatively decorate our porch and the boards over our door with it, making it seem like there had been a massacre here at some point.

It stunk like crazy at first, but now it's dried and only vaguely stinky when I get close to it. It's an excellent way to make people want to stay away. She says because it's in-betweener blood—and in-betweeners don't want to eat each other—that it won't attract them, but will also deter humans. Smart. And it worked. There are a lot of cabins around the lake, and some parts of the various developments have plenty of people in them, but we've been left alone for the most part. Our cabin isn't one of the expensive ones near the water, but rather one of the little ones close to the woods that back onto this part of the lake. The road is rutted, the parking difficult, and the amenities much further away. I'm grateful for that now. We've been left alone and alone is good at the moment.

The guy at the dock is super jumpy, but he must really need food because he's sticking it out. I'd like to go fishing too. That's out of the question if he's here.

"We'll need to go down there eventually," I say, my eyes still at the peephole.

I hear my mother sigh behind me, but she doesn't answer me immediately. Eventually, she says, "I think we will, yes, but not now. Let's just see if he's a psycho first."

*****

After a few more days of watching, I'm pretty sure he's not a psycho. I think he's just scared and alone. And really, how are we ever going to know? We could watch him forever and not be sure about it.

The bottom line for me is that we haven't caught any animals for weeks except for a few squirrels. The in-betweeners are eating them all. This area used to be thick with deer, now it's thick with deer bones. I want some fish.

"Can we go now?" I ask my mom, who has used every delaying tactic known to mom-hood. I know she doesn't feel safe—that she doesn't feel I'm safe—but she also knows we need food and fish. There are boats out on the vast waters of the lake more often lately, so I know other people are fishing too. They're probably in the same situation we're in. The stoners had a boat, but I have no idea what happened to it, only that it isn't at their dock anymore.

Our boat is far more modest—a canoe. Normally it hangs from the rafters of the cabin when we're not here in the only spot where the overhead is high enough that we won't run into it walking around. I don't know how many hours we spent on the lake inside that worn hull, my mother paddling while the cancer ate my brain. She did it just so that I could enjoy being on the water. The soothing motion made me feel better and eased my constant nausea. You'd think it would be the opposite, but chemo works differently for everyone.

Once I was well, we adventured in it, going out further and paddling harder. We even have outriggers for it so that we can relax and enjoy our trips without tipping over. Picnics on the water, my mom lying back with her hat over her eyes as the outriggers did the work of stabilizing us, the sun creating sharp glints that looked like diamonds in the water. All of it was good. I loved it.

Now, let's hope we can use it to get some food.

"Mom, the worms are going to die if we don't hurry up," I say, though I know it's not true. They are busily churning the earth in my little bucket and probably wouldn't mind at all if we didn't use them for bait.

She eyes me at those words, giving me that did-you-really-just-tell-me-that-lie look. "Really?"

"Okay, fine. But let's go," I say, tapping the canoe in the main room of the cabin with an impatient finger.

She takes a deep breath, her subconscious clearly working as she pats the gun at her hip. "You win. Let's go, but if he's a psycho, you're grounded."

I can't help that I splutter a laugh at that. Grounded? That's absurdly hilarious.

We don't go to the stoner's dock, even though it's closer, but instead to the one next to it at the Brown's cabin. We actually have a pretty cool little cart that we use to wheel the canoe out to the dock, but getting it into the water is always a pain. The shore it too rocky here and the water is too cold already to carry it out into the water.

I figure it's okay to use the Brown's dock. They never came here, so there's no reason not to get some use out of it. We already broke into their cabin and took the supplies they stocked for summer visits. So many beanie weenies.

I know the moment the guy in the stoner house sees us because he flits from window to window, lifting slats on the blinds as he tracks our progress. He's not at all sneaky about it. I think that's a good sign, really. I do feel bad that he seems afraid of us though.

My mom notices too, because she shifts her grip on the canoe, putting most of the weight on her left arm so she can draw her gun with her right if the need arises.

"Relax, Mom. He's just looking," I whisper.

"Yeah, yeah," she mutters in response and I want to giggle for some reason. It's probably nervousness, but she sounds sullen, like she always accused me of sounding when I didn't get what I wanted.

Nothing happens. There's no bullet to the back, no guy running up and asking for food, not even him coming out to look at us and give a friendly wave. Nothing.

Out on the water, I immediately feel better. So far, we've never seen an in-betweener swim. In fact, they seem a little baffled by the water. I have seen them come to the shore, bend low, and put their heads to the water, but I think they're only drinking. I was surprised to see them drinking at all, but my mom says that every animal knows to drink if it needs to. I suppose that makes sense given that they act more like animals than anything else.

The soothing sounds of the water, the little vibrations in the hull as the water laps against the sides, the feel of the smooth wooden paddle in my hands—all of it calms my nerves. I feel like I can finally take a deeper breath out here. Why didn't we do this sooner?

Once we get a little ways out, my mother gets our rods ready and puts on my worm. I don't understand the whole lure thing, but she does. I'm using a worm and she's using some crazy looking thing from her lure box. You can catch a lot of different kind of fish here, but some are easier than others. While I would rather have a nice striped bass, we'll probably wind up with a bunch of perch or bream.

It doesn't take long for me to get a bite and sure enough, I pull a wriggling white perch up for my mom to put into our bucket. It's a good sized fish for a perch, and my mouth waters as it drops into the bucket.

"You know those use to be in the Atlantic ocean, right?" she asks idly.

I've heard this before. My mom likes to make everything a lesson. I sigh.

"I've told you that before, haven't I?" she asks with a chuckle.

"You have," I answer and drop my line back into the water, a new worm wriggling on my hook.

"Then tell me what I told you," she says and gives me a wink.

"You're really going to play school with me after the end of the world?" I ask.

She nods, her hands easy on her pole and her shoulders more relaxed than I've seen in months. If for no other reason than I'd like to see her keep on feeling that way, I answer her. "When they built the dam here, the perch stuck here had to adapt or die. And they did. Even though they should want to go into the ocean, they don't. They live their whole lives here and taste very fishy."

"Anything else?" she asks, then adds, "And if you don't want them because they're too fishy, I'll be more than happy to eat your share." She winks, so I know we're still kidding.

"Hmm, aren't they something else? Like, not perch at all?" I ask.

"Yep, they're actually in the bass family," she says as she gets a bite. As she reels in her catch, my rod dips too. I can tell it's another small one, but my stomach growls all the same. We're doing well. She unhooks my fish and plops it into the bucket.

"Why do I feel like you're trying to say something else?" I ask her, because it does seem like there's some message in there.

She grins as she digs out another worm. "What do you think I'm saying? Assuming I'm not talking about fish, that is."

I think about it for a minute, but nothing comes to me. When I glance back up at her, she taps the bucket of fish casually. The bucket of perch.

Of course. I knew there had to be something important in this conversation. The perch had to adapt quickly or die without their home ocean available anymore. It seems a little too simple for one of my mom's lessons. They're usually at least two levels deep…or convoluted depending on your perspective.

"I'm adapting. I won't die," I say.

With the worm still twisting between her fingers, she tilts her head and looks me over. Finally, she says, "You are. You're amazing."

This is getting awkward, so we both get back to the business of catching fish, silent for a while until I get another bite. I'm really showing her up in terms of the fish catching. Of course, it might be simply that these fish haven't been fished all summer and are anxious for some bait. Who knows?

The shore is too far away for me to see anything as small as a person watching from a window, but I can feel the guy at the stoner house looking all the same. Or maybe it's just a case of the heebie jeebies. As my mom baits my hook again, I ask, "What do you think of the guy staying at the stoner house? You think he's a friend of theirs?"

"Don't call them stoners," my mom says, but she says it automatically. She always says that.

"Mom, they are...were...stoners. Why don't you like me saying that?"

She sighs and tosses away my hook, ready again to go and lure more fish to their deaths. Her line isn't doing what she wants—and I know she's hoping for some "good" fish so we don't just get perch—so she paws through her lure box, considering and discarding other options for her own fishing. She takes a long time to answer me.

"Emily, let me ask you this. Why do you insist on calling them stoners?"

I shrug and say, "Because they are?"

Her lips thin in disapproval and she looks out over the water. I can tell by the way she's doing it that she's trying to figure out how to tell me something, or maybe how to get across a lesson. Eventually, she looks at me and says, "First off, you know how I feel about pejoratives of any kind, and that is one, even if you don't think it is. Secondly, I think you're probably alive because of those two guys."

That shocks me. How in the world could that be possible? I don't think either of them is in the nanite business. And then it hits me. "Did you give me pot? I don't remember any pot!"

My mom rolls her eyes and says, "I put it in your smoothies."

My pole droops as I lose focus, almost dipping into the water. She reaches out to jerk it back up, but she's not meeting my eyes. I honestly think her face might be going red from embarrassment.

"You drugged me?"

Now, I'm sure she's blushing and her eyes roll heavenward. "For goodness sake, that's why I didn't tell you about it. It's not like I drugged you. I just…uh…helped you during chemotherapy. *They* helped you during your chemo."

I don't say anything because I really can't. I can't believe what I'm hearing, especially after all the talks my mom had with me about drinking, drugs, and sex when I started high school. What a hypocrite! Well, maybe not. I do remember those rank-tasting smoothies. I also remember that I stopped having trouble with nausea and food at some point too.

"It worked?" I ask, because I really have difficulty remembering some of the timelines and details of that period. Brain tumors like mine can do that.

She nods, glancing at me from the corner of her eye. "It did. I felt sort of weird about it, but it changed my mind about a few things. It changed my mind about them. Sometimes what they do helps people. They knew you needed it."

I laugh and reach out to slap her on her knee. "You are very, very cool, Mom."

She's trying to hide it, but I can see the smile on her face all the same. Yes, my mom is very cool, indeed.

*****

Our bucket is heavy with fish by the time we paddle back in. I'm starving and would like to just drop the canoe and run back to clean our catch, but there's no way we'll leave our canoe out in the open so it can disappear. Getting it onto its cart is much harder than it was to get it off. I'm tired.

And hungry for fish.

"He's looking," I whisper to my mom as she locks the strap for the cart.

She gives me a tight nod and says, "He's not very discreet."

I burst out laughing because she sounds so prim, like she's describing someone peeing in the yard at an outdoor wedding reception. My loud laugh makes her head jerk up in a panic, and that cuts it off, ruining the fun. She scowls at me and warns, "You need to cap that right now."

She's using her stern military voice, so I lose the smile entirely and say, "Sorry."

As we push the canoe, her eyes dart toward the stoner house every few steps, her head barely moving as she tries her best to keep it in view without actually turning around to gawp at it. At last, the sound of a creaking door makes her let her end of the canoe go. The boat *thunks* to the ground at my end and her end rises into the air as the cart wheels balance the middle. She whirls around with her gun out and up in a hot second.

The man from the stoner house stands on the porch with his hands in the air, his eyes so wide I can see them from here. We stand there for an eternal second and then the man waves one of his raised hands and says, "Hi."

He says it so simply that I know everything is okay. My mom apparently doesn't know that at all. The gun doesn't lower even an inch.

"Hi," I say back to him and my mom flinches at the noise.

"Don't shoot me, please," he says, very politely.

"Mom," I whisper.

That must work, because she lowers the gun, even though she doesn't holster it. The man watches my mom carefully as he lowers his hands, crossing them in front of his chest as if he's cold. My mom watches him, but doesn't raise the gun again.

I decide to break this awkward moment. It's just got to be done. This isn't neighborly at all. "Do you know them? Is that why you're here?" I ask him in a louder voice than I've used in a long time.

He looks confused until I point to the house, then he just looks uncomfortable. He coughs and says, "No, but the door was open. No one was here. Well, I think one of the owners came back, but...uh..."

"Was he wearing a yellow shirt?" I break in when he trails off.

He starts and nods. "He was."

"Yep, he owned the place. Him and another guy, but the other one is already dead. The guy in the yellow shirt ate him," I say and it strikes me how very odd this conversation is. My life has changed so much it's hard to believe this is even really the same life sometimes.

"Did you take care of him? The yellow shirt?" my mom asks.

The man looks away again. His voice is a little rough when he answers. "I did. I had to."

"Good," my mom says and shoves her gun into her holster.

The man glances at our canoe and clears his throat. "Don't take this the wrong way, but can I ask if you caught fish? I'm not asking for them, only asking if you caught some."

My mom's lips purse, but she answers. "We did."

"I haven't been able to catch any," he says.

"You have to go a little further out this time of year. Rob and Tom—the guys who owned this place—have a boat, but it's gone. They should have kayaks in their cabin though. Use those," she says. She's starting to look around again. We're making too much noise and there are in-betweeners in these woods. More every day.

The man notices and says, "Okay. Thank you." He looks disappointed, sort of hopeless.

My mom reaches for her end of the canoe, but I put up my hand for her to wait and ask, "Do you know how to use a kayak?"

We're not close enough for me to be sure, but I think the man's eyes are reddening, like he's about to cry. His voice confirms that when he answers me. It's thick and full. "No. I've never been on one in my life. I've never been in a boat."

My mom's shoulders are all tight and hunched again. She won't look at him. Instead, she glares at me and I know that means we're going.

"I'm sorry," I say and put my hands to the boat.

As we go, I think I hear him sadly say, "Me too."

*****

The fish smell divine. Perch are not my favorite and that's what most of our catch today consists of. Despite that, my mouth is so full of slobber I feel like I might actually drool if I open my mouth. We've got some fish breading and dried milk—but no eggs—so the fillets are now crispy and brown, just like I like them.

I'm ready to dig in, relishing the idea of eating my fill without thoughts past saving some for breakfast. Yet my mother is standing there with that big plate piled high with fish and looking at it instead of putting it on the little table in the cabin.

I pick up my fork and spoon in my fists and stand them up to either side of my plate in a way meant to be comedic and say, "Feed me, Seymour!"

"What?" she murmurs, finally looking up from her little daze. Then she smiles and says, "Oh. Yes, I'll bet you're ready." She puts the dish on the table, but she still doesn't sit down to eat. I fork a fillet and drop it onto my plate. It makes a very satisfying sound as it hits the ceramic.

"Mom, what's wrong," I say, my excitement over the fish fading as she stands there staring at the plate. I have no idea what's going on, but I don't think it can be good if it involves scowling at the food I'm about to feast on.

Instead of answering, she sucks in a deep breath and grabs another plate out of the rack. "Dag blast it," she mutters and begins forking fillets onto the plate. She takes about a quarter of them while I look on in dismay.

"What are you doing?" I ask her, ready to put my hand over the plate because I've just figured out what she's probably up to. "Are you taking him our fish?"

She nods, her face grim. "I might be an idiot, but if we can't keep acting like decent humans, then what's the point?" She stops taking fillets, tosses the fork onto the table, and says, "Tell me I'm not an idiot for doing this. Tell me this is the right thing to do."

My mom is not often uncertain, but she is now. She's probably worried this will make the man leech onto us, or turn on us, or do something else awful. People have been doing terrible things to each other since this started, so it's not an illogical thing to worry might happen. But she's right. This is, without a shred of doubt, the right thing to do.

"Go," I say. "You want backup?"

She shakes her head and pats the gun at her side with her free hand. "I'm good. I really don't think he's dangerous. But watch from the front anyway."

As she walks toward the stoner cabin with a plate of fish in her hand, I watch her. I get the feeling we'll be teaching him how to kayak soon, maybe even teaching him how to fish. I'm so proud that she's my mom.

Today – Date with the Dead

The buzz of the alarm clock is so alien that I wake up in a panic, grabbing for my crossbow and sliding into the corner of the room before I'm even truly awake. When I realize what it is, I laugh, congratulate myself on having a decent reaction time, and then shut it off.

The first thing I want to do is see what might have happened at the fence during the rest of the night. If too many deaders have gathered—especially after the ruckus last night—then I'll have a hard time getting out of the gate, and the gate is the only way out. The other gate has been blocked since shortly after my mother and I got here. She pulled a big truck up in front of the gate in a series of dangerously out-of-control jerks and it's been sitting there ever since, tires flat and tanks long since drained of fuel.

It takes only a little time to get ready and I fill up on cold rice—this time skipping the leftover canned tomatoes. All my gear is waiting for me, laid out in an orderly line and ready for me to go through my checklist one more time. I wrote a note before the last of the light died yesterday and as I leave the room, I use a precious bit of duct tape to affix it to the door of the office. It's an invitation to anyone who might stumble onto this place to enjoy the sanctuary it provides, along with information on where they can find various necessities.

I thought long and hard about whether or not to leave this note. It's been a long time since anyone came by this place, so the chances of it happening while I'm gone—assuming I come back—are probably close to nil. But if I don't return, I'd rather someone use it and not wonder if somebody more aggressive is planning on returning.

There's a second note in my pocket, this one with information on how to find this place. I won't carry it, Sam will. I'm hoping that, if I don't make it, Sam will be coherent enough to know to give this note to the kids he's working so hard to protect. It's the best I can do. In a way, I suppose it's like my last will and testament, and for some reason I feel comforted by the idea of that.

Before I pull the car out, I go to the edge of the buildings and take a peek at the front gate and fence. Sam is there, his mouth around a rail and a wide swath of red running from his mouth, over his neck, and probably soaking his shirt, though I can't see that for sure from here. That's one of the downsides of wanting metals. They tear up their mouths something fierce. It's rare to see a deader with their teeth intact. More often, they have a mouth full of sharp and broken shards. Tongues suffer too, as does any other soft mouth tissue.

The rest of him looks a little worse for wear too. I can see the darker color along his side where the little in-betweener got to him. I still don't understand why she attacked him like she did. The deaders don't seem to want to eat him, so I wonder if maybe that little one was just too small to make it as an in-betweener. Maybe her behavior was simply out of character for them. But, and this is a big consideration, it might simply be that Sam is too different, too close to human.

There are still at least a dozen deaders attached to the gate. Some must have wandered off during the night, perhaps attracted by a disturbance somewhere else. A dozen is too many for me to open the gate safely. It opens inward and they'll come right along with it, focusing on me the minute I get within range of whatever they can sense me with.

I drive the car around the corner and don't even bother to slow down, bumping up onto the grassy field and right up to the fence where Sam is still tied. At the sight of the car, he ceases his licking and goes in-betweener on me, following the car's motion with predatory eyes and snapping jaws. A ripple of motion goes through the deaders at the gate at the vibrations my car sends through the ground, but once I stop the car, they gradually go back to their rails.

I sit in the car for a minute, watching Sam as he watches me, waiting to see if he's too far gone or if he's going to be able to get control of himself. He's been out here a long time and he's probably hungry. I've got a solution for that.

Hopping out of the car, I grab the sack on the seat next to me and waste no time. Sam is making noises, frustrated and hungry ones, and I've got to stop him before I get more company. I toss a bird carcass his way, but it bounces off the rails. He couldn't grab for it anyway with his hands tied, but it does what I wanted. It draws his attention. His nostrils flare and he jerks his head around like an animal scenting something very nice.

I take out a second one, and this time, hold it in my hand until his eyes lock on it. Once I've got his full attention focused on my outstretched hand, I step close and hold it to the side, so that his eyes follow its progress. I reach out quickly and shove my snippers between his wrists, cut the zip tie, then toss the feathery carcass in a slow underhand throw over the fence.

He reflexively turns to follow the path of the bird, then scrambles for it when it hits the ground with a pitiful thud. He sits down on the ground and tears into it. It's a pretty bird, some sort of dove, I think. Gray with black and white, and even a hint of soft pink, it also has a rounded head and gentle eyes. It's one of my favorite kinds. Their strange cooing sounds sad and beautiful and it comforts me when things get bad.

My sack is heavy with their bodies, along with several pigeons. They had no fear of me, seeming only confused when my arrows started to bring them down from the roof. I feel a tear slip down my face and wipe it away impatiently. I eat the birds sometimes, though I've never taken them from my roof before. I'm not sure why it feels like this, but it does. It's like I've broken some promised sanctuary for them.

When he's done, his face is covered with the remains of the bird, feathers stuck to him like he's trying to be funny. They flutter when his head whips around toward me again. I toss over another, then another, and we keep on like this while the sun rises in the sky and he fills whatever strange need the in-betweeners have that requires so much fresh, raw flesh.

After about a dozen birds, he stops eating suddenly. He's still sitting splay-legged on the ground, his head bent over the last bird I sent over the fence. He lowers his hands, now more feathery gore than anything else, and seems to be looking at them. I wonder for a moment if some new stage of in-betweener behavior is about to start when he looks up at me. In his eyes are disbelief, disgust, and pain, directed not at me, but at himself. I'm sure of that.

To be an in-betweener has got to be horrible. It's something I've thought about. If I think it's going to happen to me and there's no hope, I'm pretty sure my decision will be to blow my head entirely off with a double-barreled shotgun blast to the head. It might not work, but obliterating the head is the one way I know of to ensure the deaders and in-betweeners truly die. And I won't have to worry about noise at that point.

But to be an in-betweener and understand what you are must be the worst possible fate of all. And I think that's exactly what has happened to Sam.

He drops the bird and wipes his hands down his face. It's awkward and looks more like a slap, but he manages to wipe off a good bit of the mess. Then he drags his hands across the ground, wiping them as well. When he regains his feet, I have to admit that he does look healthier under all the dirt and bloody bits. His color is better—where I can see it—and his face almost seems plumper, like a dehydrated person after drinking their fill.

"Are you with me, Sam?"

He starts at my voice, but doesn't rush the fence or anything like that. He grunts a little, like he's testing his voice, then says, "Go."

It's the clearest word I've heard him say. Maybe it's the birds, but he seems very lucid. I hope he's up for the rest of what I need him to do.

"I can't get the gate open with them there. Can you help me get rid of them?" I ask, pointing to the gate and the deaders congregated there.

He bounces on his knees a little, but also nods his head, so I'm even more convinced he's thinking clearly after his feast of birds. It seems the letter from Veronica about feeding was right about more than just keeping him a little tamer.

I wait to see what he'll do next. I don't have to wait long. He looks at the deaders, then at me, then he shrugs. I take the shrug to mean he's looking for some instruction on how to accomplish what I want. The way he tossed that deader into the car was great, but there aren't enough empty cars along the street for him to do that with all of the deaders. My problem is that I can take care of them if I have time and can get out of the gate for head smashing, but with Sam around, I can't take that kind of time and I for sure can't go outside my fences. I have to keep my weapons ready to bear against Sam as much as any of them.

I open the hatch of my car and pull out a rope I've already prepared. I was thinking I might have to do this myself, at best maybe using him to distract the deaders, but if he can stay like he is right now, I have a much better idea. If he's this lucid, why not use it and speed our progress at the same time.

He's watching me, so I toss one of the loops over my head and tighten it a little around my neck. Then I motion as if I'm putting the next loop around another neck. "Do you understand?"

"Ya," he says and holds out his hands.

Once he has the rope, he doesn't hesitate. He walks right up to the deaders, pulls one off the fence, and cinches the first loop around the thing's neck. There are a few extra loops, but I'm okay with extra. When he's done, he has eleven fairly docile deaders lined up and roped. It's more difficult to get him to understand that the final loop on the end needs to go over one of the spikes at the top of the fence away from the gate, but we eventually get it worked out. There's one moment of worry on my part when he climbs onto the brick base and reaches for the top finials, but he seems to be much more capable of control this morning. It's a good data point, even if I do have to kill him again later.

The gate is clear, but the next part is a bit tricky. I'm not sure he'll go for it. From the car's hatch I withdraw a dog-catcher I took from the vet hospital. It's just a long metal pole with a plastic-covered braided wire looped at the end that I can tighten or loosen at the other end. I know they have some sort of official name, but I don't know it, so dog-catchers they are. I have several, but I can only handle one at a time. I'd like to have a few extra arms so I could hold him with more, but I've just got the two. I could just leave him behind and go on my own, but I know what *I* would do if someone I didn't know came sauntering up to this place.

People aren't safe.

If I have Sam with me, then they'll know he's the one who brought me the note. It's entirely possible that they've never seen me, that only he has, and that's why they sent him. Even if not, they're kids and probably very jumpy after losing their only remaining guardian. And I haven't forgotten that the note said he had been shot by accident. I'd prefer no further accidents, particularly when it's me that could wind up like Sam in the course of the accident.

He retreats from the fence when he spies the dog-catcher. I wasn't sure he'd know what it was—and I don't think he does, really—but some memory is tickling at him because he frowns and holds out his hands as if to distance himself from me and my crazy tool.

I show him how it works by putting it around my neck and holding out the pole. "This is just to be sure I can be safe with you. That's all. I promise I won't hurt you," I say.

This close, I can really see his face. His eyes are gray, the lashes around them so thick and dark that it almost looks like he's wearing eyeliner. He has the exact kind of eyes I'd expect to see looking back out from the pages of a glossy magazine. Except, they're also bloodshot and crusted with goop at the corners, which definitely kills the whole attraction thing.

We look at each other for a moment and the breeze shifts so that it flows from my direction toward him. Sam's face goes feral again, his nose lifting to sniff the air. He lowers his head a little, staring at me like a rabid dog ready to lunge.

"Sam! Stay with me!" I snap.

His head jerks and a growl comes out of him that's low and scary. I lift the crossbow and aim for the space between the bars of the gate. Only the gate is between us and he could climb that pretty fast if he wanted. He's tall, in great shape, and full of that in-betweener rage at the moment. I can probably get to the car before he catches me, but there's no one to drop the door for me at the furniture warehouse. I'd have to play chase with him around the complex until I could get the drop on him or until he got it on me.

If I can't calm him, I'll have to kill him and take my chances with the kids.

Then I remember the bag of leftover birds. It's less than twenty feet from me. Can I get to it and get one out before he makes his move? Seven big strides equals about twenty feet. Twenty feet never seemed like such a long distance before.

"Sam, I've got more birds. Just hang on!" I yell and sidestep toward the bag on the ground.

I don't take my eyes off of him for a second and my crossbow is pointed at his head the entire time. A single shot is unlikely to kill him, but it will disturb his ability to process information. If I'm lucky, a shot through the brain will hit something that he needs to remain mobile and cause one of those overdrive reactions. But I've shot some with three or four bolts and had them keep lurching along, so I'd rather not chance it.

As he did yesterday, he makes that horrible keening noise and starts beating at his head. He stumbles in a small circle, his fists making thuds against his skull even I can hear. Snatching the bag, I let my crossbow dangle from my shoulder, rip open the top of the bag, and sink my fingers into the unpleasantly cool carcasses. I throw my handful over the fence directly in Sam's direction. At the motion, his head whips up. The presence of fresh food does what I had hoped and he makes for the little bodies.

He doesn't even bother to sit down this time, merely taking small steps around the litter of bodies as if he needs to keep them in view. I toss over all the remaining birds—seven in total—and then watch as he eats.

If he can only keep himself in check for an hour or so after each meal, then how am I going to control him for the entire trip? And there's no time for me to go shoot more. Getting this many took forever yesterday and I was only able to do it because the light was dimming and they were settling down for the evening on the roofs. In the bright light of day, they'll just fly away. Plus, they probably don't trust me anymore.

Then again, he went without feeding for most of the day and all night. Who knows how long it was before then that he ate. It's possible that he's just catching up. I'm being far too optimistic and I know it, but I really don't want to get shot by some nervous kids.

Sam finally finishes, goes through the same wiping process he did before, but he looks a lot less appalled by his actions this time. I'm not sure if that's good or bad.

He stands up and at the sound of my feet on the drive, he turns. His fists clench, but he says, "Ya," and glances down at the dog-catcher at my feet.

I'm still not sure this is such a good idea. When he sidles up and sticks his clenched fists through the gap between two rails in the gate, I move forward with my zip ties as if he's the one in charge. With his wrists bound, he lets them fall to his waist. I stick the dog-catcher through the fence and slip the loop over his head.

Now I have him. Useful for keeping an angry dog out of reach, the dog-catcher also works splendidly for deaders and now, in-betweeners. At least they do in theory. The reality is that Sam is much bigger and stronger than I am. If he really wanted to get away from me, I doubt I could stop him with this.

After a quick look around, I open the gate—carefully maneuvering the dog-catcher's handle so that I can keep him away from me as I shift my grip—then lead Sam to the car. There's a pull cord I've rigged up using some rope and I hook it up to the dog-catcher pole while I stand at the back of the car and wonder what the hell kind of stupidity this whole idea is.

After that, I have my only moment of real vulnerability. The pull cord goes from the end of the dog-catcher into the back hatch of the car and through the dog fence, then trails out the driver's side door. I have no idea if this will work. I reach down and grab the cord, pulling in the slack as fast as I can while keeping a good grip on the dog-catcher.

It jerks Sam almost off his feet and toward the back of the car when I finally get the last of the slack out. He goes compliantly enough and doesn't do more than wail softly when I yank on the cord to get the end of the pole through the dog fence. There's no resistance from him and he goes into the hatch with only a few bumps and bangs. Tossing in the pull cord, I tie it to the seat just to make myself feel better.

It takes every ounce of willpower I have to get in the driver's seat. Sam's face is pressed against the window behind my seat.

"This is so stupid," I say and get into the car.

Fifteen Months Ago – Programming Futility

We've found a warehouse complex that seems like it has barely been looted at all. It's amazing. After living off whatever food we can scavenge from vending machines and desk drawers, along with the back-of-the-cabinet food we find in the occasional apartment, I feel like we've hit the lottery.

Having a full belly is an unbelievable luxury. It's hard to imagine how I took it so for granted before. But, I did. We all did. I used to say I didn't like beans of any sort, and lima beans were like poison. If you gave me a pristine can of limas today, I'd do the happy dance and be grateful for the gift.

Even the lake seems like a distant past filled with luxury. The fish from the lake, the warmth of a familiar bed, the sound of my mom doing dishes while I slept late in the morning. All of that is gone now. Gone for good, most likely. When the in-betweeners showed up in force, it was all we could do to escape with our packs and our car. We got lucky.

So yeah, this place is like heaven on earth to me now that I've known how bad it can get. I understand hunger in a way I never did before. And there is so much food here.

"Mom, I'm going to do rounds, maybe practice my bow for a while. That okay?" I ask.

She taps a few more times on her tablet, frowns at what she sees there, then looks up at me blankly.

"Rounds. Bow practice. Okay?" I repeat.

She nods, going back to her tablet, then looks back up at me and says, "Stay within the drop-off zone, okay? Don't get within view of the street or the field. Got it?"

"Sure, no problem," I assure her, zipping up my coat and tugging on some gloves.

She means the big circle of asphalt in the center of this group of warehouses where trucks were loaded and unloaded. There's employee parking adjoining it and that's where I've got the targets for my bow practice set up. It's a good space. Only between the buildings are we visible from beyond the fence. Even then, because of the way the complex is landscaped, there are trees and bushes that provide decent cover between buildings. Best of all, the fence is as far from the drop-off zone as any place in the entire compound, which means anyone passing on the street—dead or alive—can't see anyone out there.

My mom is still looking at me with her brow furrowed. The lines between her eyebrows are so deep they look black from where I stand. I know she has something to say.

"What?" I ask.

Her mouth opens, then closes again. The lines smooth a little and she puts on a smile so fake it would be funny in a different situation. Finally, she simply says, "I love you, honey."

"I love you too," I say.

She looks small sitting on the concrete floor near the open warehouse door, strangely diminished from the woman who once strode around like she owned the world. And I don't mean shrunken from the weight loss or the rapid aging brought about by too many sleepless nights and endless days filled with fear. It's more like she's shrinking under the weight of all that's happened.

Especially since she holds at least some responsibility for it happening in the first place.

On impulse, I walk over and bend to kiss her cheek. It's cool and her skin feels papery thin against my lips. She smiles up at me and this time it's a real one, though wan and tired. I slide down the wall to sit next to her and rest my head on her shoulder. It's not like I have a schedule to keep or anything. I'm in no hurry. We did our daily rounds this morning as we always do, so I have no real reason to do them again. Mostly, I just want to go look at the food again and loose a few arrows at the target.

"How's that going?" I ask, nodding toward the tablet propped up on her legs.

She sighs and I can tell her mind is shifting back to work again. It's selfish of me, but I'm actually glad of that. When she's absorbed in this project of hers, no matter how futile I may think it is, I can get a little peace. When she's not working on that, she's worrying about me or doing more work than any one person can reasonably be expected to do.

She does so much because she doesn't want me exposed to what's going on outside any more than I have to be. It's only been since we came here and developed a routine that she's really allowed me to participate in the activities that keep us safe. I hunted with her at the lake, went fishing, and kept watch during the day when things were quiet, but when something bad had to be done, she always did it. And did it as far from me as she could so I wouldn't see.

Since we got here, she seems to have come to some sort of decision within herself. It's like she suddenly realized that this isn't going to end, at least not anytime soon, and that I'll need to know how to take care of myself if I want to survive. She even lets me go with her on rounds while she takes care of the in-betweeners who have become something else.

I'm not entirely sure what's happening there, but a lot of the in-betweeners are failing. They don't die, but they become something else. They're slow, not as dangerous, but also exceedingly nasty.

She's teaching me the things I *really* need to know in this world. Like how to most effectively bash a deader into oblivion, how to maintain our perimeter, and how to quickly shift my aim if a human turns out to be an in-betweener. She's even letting me take watch at night now. I've been able to use a crossbow against the deaders that stumble down the street or wander in the field beyond the fence. She allowed me to practice with the crossbow right from the start, but she rarely let me use it against the deaders or in-betweeners until we got here. She wanted to spare me, I know, but it just made me feel useless. It made me feel like I was dead weight.

And now I feel useful and I like it. So, I like to encourage her on her project just to be sure she stays busy and I can stay useful. I nudge her with my elbow and nod toward the computer again.

She lowers the screen a little and sighs. "I don't know. Unless someone can actually test this, it's useless. And all I have is this computer. There's no linkup. I've not caught even a sniff of an internet connection since the lake. But..." She trails off, biting at her lip and looking at the screen.

"But?" I prod.

"I think I might have something here," she says. The way she says it—that hint of triumph hiding inside the uncertainty—draws my full attention. Her eyes lift to mine again, her brows twitching upward and an undeniable light shining in her eyes. That light is one I haven't seen since all of this started.

Now, I'm interested.

"Wait, what? Really? As in, something that can fix this?"

The victorious hint is snuffed out, just like that. With an uncertain shake of her head, she says, "It's going to be hard to fix everything, but this," she pauses and pokes her finger at an undecipherable line of code on the screen, "is a start. It's manual, not remote, but it could work."

"Can we do it?" I ask.

What I mean is can we—her and me—do this from within the relative safety of this complex of warehouses? It's an idyll filled with never-to-be-sold office furniture, mountains of floral sachets, and a warehouse full of Indian, Latin, and Chinese food meant for the international grocery stores. On the downside, it's without power like everywhere else, and we only have a few scavenged bits of portable solar to create electricity with, the kind meant to charge portable electronics while camping or during outages. That's enough for her computer and my music player, but not much more.

"No, baby. I need nanites to do this. But, this code could work on a whole host of digesting nanite types. There should be plenty of nanite cores at any location where nanite treatment was done." She looks back down at her code on the screen and adds, "There might be billions—heck, trillions or more—of them in storage, just waiting for someone to load a program into the formatting machines."

I think of the military hospital, with an entire wing dedicated to nanite treatment. I think of the long hallways of isolation rooms where those being treated stayed while their nanites did their work. I think of the rooms filled with techno-magical equipment used to program, check, and then deliver nanites to the masses that surged through the doors every day.

"It's a long way, but we could get there," I offer tentatively.

She knows where I mean, because she turns the tablet over, making its screen go dark, and swivels on the floor to face me. Her hands grip mine hard, not so hard that it goes into painful territory, but close.

"No. That's more than eighty miles and there are only two of us. I have no way to save this data on anything other than this drive. Aside from the significant factor that if we don't make it, this drive will be lost forever, I have no intention of losing you—a far more significant factor that I have to consider. You're the most important person in this world to me and a trip like that would be almost guaranteed to fail with only two people and so many deaders and their ugly half-dead cousins between us and the base."

She licks her lips and her eyes dart around like she's expecting a bunch of deaders to show up at the door. Sometimes, she gets like that. It happens less now that we've been safe here for a while, with all the deaders cleared from inside the fence, but it still happens.

With a deep breath, she calms herself, brings her system down from that wound-up tenseness she winds herself up into. Her eyes are clear and focused when she opens them again. She says, "No, we'll wait for the military to start expanding its territory again. Or for anyone official at all to show up in this area. We'll hand it off when it's safe to do that. The risks are too great that it will never make it there otherwise. And, anyway, I'm not entirely sure about it yet. I need to work on it more."

I nod, but say nothing. She wouldn't be so firm about saying we shouldn't go if she was sure that we shouldn't do exactly that. When she's positive about a course of action, she just says it and that's that. It's only when my mom *isn't* sure that she gets like this, almost like she's trying to convince herself of the right path to take.

It was the same when the trickle of in-betweeners around the lake turned into a stream, then a flood, and we had to leave. And again when the law offices we were holed up in became untenable because all the nearby resources ran out.

Both times she was emphatic about going or staying until we really did need to go, and then she was calm and quiet.

Her fingers dance along the back of the tablet, like she's already busy tapping out code trapped in her brain. I know she wants to get back to work. And I'd like to go and look at the food. She reassures herself by working on her nanite program. I do it by counting packets of saffron rice. We all have our crutches these days.

At least we're still breathing.

Today – Driving Without A License

With Sam inside the car, so close to me that I can smell his overpowering carrion stench, I almost panic and get out of the car again. The idea that I should take a nap and pretend none of this ever happened is a powerful one. Bathing in the smell of blood and whatever it is that he's done in his pants is just driving the idea home with a little extra force. Even taking deep breaths to calm down isn't an option because the smell is making me gag.

I absolutely have to turn on the AC—which is a big use of energy I'll probably need later—and blow as much air as I can away from me and toward him. I've drawn out a sketch of the streets I'll need, along with lots of alternatives. I'm hopeful that most of my path will allow a skinny car like this one through.

The world didn't go to hell entirely overnight. Most people at least had time to run out of gas somewhere or hole up for days. Or months. When my mom and I were looking for this place, we had very little trouble getting through the streets, though we did attract some attention that required a great deal of shooting on my mom's part. I can't imagine that it would be too much worse now on the roads. No one has been driving around to get stuck, that's for sure.

It feels weird to be driving. Actually, I have to fight the impulse to look over my shoulder because I don't have my license. It's stupid, I know, but there it is.

Also, I'm a very bad driver.

There's a sad and very forlorn look to the city as I get closer. I'm sticking to the main thoroughfare through town, which is no better than any other route. I could make an argument for there being people to see me on any stretch of road, really.

If I use a main street, I run the risk of being seen by survivors downtown, where the buildings are dense and the advantage lies with anyone who views me from above. Then again, there's not much in the way of food left in town—I know because we had to leave the law offices once there was nothing left to scavenge—and smart survivors would have headed somewhere they could grow or find food.

On the other hand, if I take the long circuitous route to avoid downtown, I'll go right past the suburbs where smart survivors would have gone and turned lawns into gardens. Lower density buildings, but longer sightlines would make me just as visible to anyone with bad intentions who wants to interfere with me.

So, all things considered, the easiest and fastest route seems like the best choice. If I can get through quickly, then even if someone sees us, they might not have time to follow.

Those first miles are the longest of my life. I feel more tension and fright during that drive than I did walking alone to find medicine for my mother, more than when I went with her around our area to see how populated it was after we found the industrial park, more than that first day when we left our home forever. Sam is behind me, alternately mashing his face against the barrier as if he wants to get at me and huddling at the back, hitting himself and making noises.

It's far more distracting than driving with a cell phone. Or texting. And those were both big no-no's.

I pass the hulking wrecks of a grocery store, a strip mall, and assorted businesses, and then we're downtown. Everything here is crammed together and on each succeeding block the buildings reach a little higher into the sky than the last. The apartments over the storefronts look ominous to me, the windows in shadow capable of hiding a multitude of peering faces.

At every point where I need to make a turn, I stop and look. I've read enough dark and gritty end-of-times fiction to know the drill. Bad guys always create a roadblock out of cars or something and then swarm you. That's how it goes. But the breakdown of order has been different in some ways than in novels I've read.

For one thing, there aren't that many abandoned cars in the roads. Most people went home and watched the news when it started. That shifted to staying home and hiding. At least it did for the people who were marginally smart. Very few went driving around once the in-betweeners started in.

Before the power went out for good and we could still pick up broadcasts, there were lots of images of people running around the streets, but it was always the same people who wind up looting or burning things when anything goes wrong. Those, plus the groups of people who seemed to think bashing in-betweeners was a game. Then those people inevitably became in-betweeners themselves because no matter how much fun they thought it would be to go bashing heads, it wasn't a game.

It took time for things to get like they are now.

My mom and I cleared out of the suburbs and our house—with its expanses of easily broken glass—fast. Faster than most, for sure. By the time we headed back into the suburbs after fleeing the lake, the world was like this. Our house had been burned along with the rest of the homes on our street and everything was so different that it didn't even seem like the same universe. Things weren't exactly like this, because back then there were uncountable in-betweeners and far fewer deaders, but this hellish landscape is what we returned to.

It's not hard to picture what caused much of the carnage we pass. Little wagons meant to carry children at play lay turned over, their ruined contents spilled around them. Trash cans have been tossed about, as if to slow down a pursuer. And, as always, the picked over remains of people are everywhere I look. There are always lots and lots of those, but there aren't any fresh ones and that's an encouraging sign. And to top it all off, two years' worth of trash has been blown out of all the broken windows and scattered everywhere, just to make things especially untidy looking.

I finally see something that resembles my literary imaginings. Up ahead, at a corner where I have to either turn or not, is something decidedly out of place. It looks like the tail ends of two demolished police cars were parked back to back, as if to block an oncoming vehicle. The scorched remains of a semi-truck is pushed between them, clearly crashed. It doesn't look like a trap so much as a law enforcement action gone awry, but I'm not taking chances. I detour around the scene, traveling an extra two blocks before turning.

Aside from birds, I don't see another living thing. Nothing. No cats, no dogs, not one single thing other than me and the in-betweener growling in the back of my car. There's no noise either. I put my driver's-side window down and ditch the AC because the smell is so incredibly bad, but all I hear are the sounds of the wind and startled birds.

It might be strange for me to think this, but it's actually sort of peaceful in a grim way. The way the blinds clatter inside broken windows, the sound of a rusty can rolling first one way and then another in the breeze, and how the birds swoop from building to building—it's all oddly beautiful.

During that first year, when the in-betweeners outnumbered the deaders and filled the world with their chaotic and destructive behavior, it felt like the chaos would never end. We grew so used to being quiet and careful that living in silence began to seem natural. For a while there, I wanted more than anything just to hear a person speak in a normal tone of voice.

Now, another year has passed and far fewer humans remain alive, meaning fewer potential recruits to replenish the ranks of the in-betweeners. The in-betweeners out there are going deader and the deaders are descending into stillness from lack of food. So the chaos is sporadic and rare once again. That makes it almost peaceful. Almost.

Once we enter the college area, things pick up a little. There's more green space here. Untended parks in sore need of maintenance, big unmown swaths of grass where college kids used to lounge, and gardens gone to seed behind some of the swankier buildings provide habitat for animals. And animals mean food. Squirrels under siege, as it were.

A few shambling deaders lurch about the area, heads turning in our direction just a few seconds too late. They don't even have the energy left to hurry after us. In the distance, I hear the distinctive keening wail of an in-betweener. It's brief and cuts off abruptly. It's almost like a hunting call with them, some instinctive response to the sight of prey. At least, that's what I used to think. Now that I've seen Sam doing it in what I can only describe as pain, I'm not so sure.

Our college is old, as in *venerably* old. There's a lot of wrought iron and dozens of old carriage stanchions left over as reminders of the more gracious days of horse-drawn carriages. No-longer-mobile deaders lie in piles around them, a few still moving sluggishly at the disturbance created by my passing car.

What I see is encouraging. My mother said that the updates wouldn't allow the nanites to last forever, no matter how persistent they made the nanites and their little nanite factories. Eventually, the systems would shut down, the host flesh too decayed to respond to the nanites' frantic need to repair the damage, while still securing materials for their own maintenance.

There would be an ever-lowering response to an ever-increasing need inside the bodies of those who host nanites. And without spreading first to another host, that means the nanites will eventually be gone. Mere molecules joining the earth and of no harm to anyone.

She said we just needed to hang on long enough for these things that used to be people to die off. And it looks like that's happening. In my area, they're hanging on better because there is more food in nature. Here, where the city displaces nature, they're dying—for real.

I don't see any in-betweeners and I've heard only the one call. I wonder at that a little. They are mobile and use whatever of their brain is left to them. I imagine that most leave areas like this in their search for food. That might be why I see more of them where I live, being so close to the woods and the farms beyond. The rodents at old farms beyond my area are probably a good source of food for them.

The streets narrow and the maze of one-way streets begins. Just the idea of trying to navigate my way around this place when I eventually started college used to intimidate me. I missed going to college by two years.

At least I'll never have to worry about paying back student loans or sending my mom into debt to pay tuition. And bonus—no traffic cops! I pay no attention to the one-way street signs and keep my eyes peeled for traps. Again, there is nothing. Just more devastation and decay.

I find the block where the address is and Sam gets agitated again. The pole connected to his neck loop jerks around in the space between the two front seats, banging into the windshield with such force that I worry he's going to break it. I see signs of his former habitation here. There's a fairly mobile deader tied to a streetlight, the neck a mass of scars and missing flesh. There are more bodies, deaders now bashed into oblivion. Some of them are old, dried out or rotted to mere bones. Others are newer. We're close.

And there it is. The building is not at all what I expected. Remembering the grand old houses divided up into apartments that are the bread and butter of the college apartment experience, that's what I expected. Instead, in front of me stands a perfectly square block of loft apartments, meant to appear post-industrial, but only managing to look pretentious.

Recessed areas allowing for balconies tell me that there is one apartment to each side of the centerline on each floor. There's probably the same setup on the back side. That would be twenty apartments. Too many. And there are businesses on the bottom floor, a coffee place and the usual deli-slash-sandwich shop.

"Coffee," I whisper, then shake my head. No time for scavenging coffee beans, even if there are any to scavenge. If he lived here, Sam probably got the coffee a long time ago if the looters didn't. But even the notion of going in and sniffing any empty bags that might still smell of beans is enough to make my heart beat a little faster.

I look back at Sam. He's pressed up against the window, looking at the building's upper floors. When I follow his line of sight, it seems like he's looking at the top floor or the one below. That makes sense. If it were me stuck in this area, I'd live on one of the top floors as well.

"Well, there's no time like the present," I say, softly.

Thirteen Months Ago – Studying Death

"Okay, time for school," my mom says, hefting a three-pound sledgehammer and putting the handle through the loop at her belt. She's got a deader hooked to the fence with a loop of wire, a length of pipe attached to the wire keeping it in place. This is what she's using for show-and-tell today.

We've been getting a surge of deaders into our area lately. Every morning when we make the rounds, there are at least a dozen of them at various points along the perimeter. And at the gate, there can be as many as a full dozen more. My mom has been adamant that I not do much in the way of dispatching the deaders, but the work is just too much for her to do alone anymore.

"So, what stage would you put this one at? And what does this deader tell you about where it might have come from and how it came to be here?"

"Mom, I don't see why that's important. I really don't want to know anything about them. Let's just get rid of them," I say, gesturing with my own sledge at the corpse at the fence. It keeps reaching out for my mom with its one remaining hand, the fingers like animated sticks they're so withered. It's a really gross one and I don't even want to get near it. I can't tell her that, though. She's finally going to teach me, let me be more than a passenger in this endless flight of ours.

She sighs, deeply and with suppressed irritation, and shoots a level look my way that I take to mean I'm being difficult.

"Emily. Ask yourself this question. Why are we suddenly getting more deaders here?" she asks, knocking down the deader's reaching hand again. I can't suppress a shiver at that. How can she bear to just smack its hand down like that? Gross.

"I don't know. Because it's summer? Deaders are out of school and going on vacation?" I ask and shrug.

When she answers, each word is clearly enunciated like I'm trying her patience, which—to be completely fair here—I think I might be doing. "Because wherever they were before is no longer supporting them and they are seeking food. And look at the condition of them. Something is going on. Wouldn't you say that's something we might be more than a little curious about?"

Ah, so this *is* important. I totally didn't get that.

"Alright, got it," I say and turn to really look at the deader. For the most part, I try to avoid looking too carefully at their features or anything about them that might make me see remnants of their former humanity. It's too hard to smash their heads if I start thinking of them that way.

Swallowing, I look at the deader's face. This one was female if the clothes are any indication. The ragged remains of a T-shirt emblazoned with a movie logo popular with the teen girl set hangs from its skinny frame. I was a huge fan of that series of books and movies too. It looks like this girl and I were both rooting for the same boy to get the girl in the end. It's very weird to realize that. The long hair sort of reinforces the notion of it being a girl, though now hunks of scalp are missing and what's left of the hair is a snarled mess of leaves, twigs, and assorted debris I'd rather not know much about. She also smells incredibly bad.

She's got no eyes, which is fairly normal for one this bad off, and her entire face from just below the nose to the chin is a raw and ragged mess from licking and sucking metal. She has no front teeth at all. The missing arm was torn off at the elbow and the wound hasn't healed at all. The wound also looks very dry. My guess is that her arm got torn off after she went deader and the nanite repairs slowed down substantially.

As far as what killed her? That's obvious, even in the condition she's in. The neat slice across her neck healed over after she was revived. The area is covered with the typical weird, bumpy tissue that nanites stimulate the skin to develop.

"She's been like this a while, I'd say. Someone cut her throat and I think that's what killed her. So, it was a human who killed her or she did it herself. Her clothes aren't practical for being on the run, so I'd guess she was killed while in hiding or very early on," I say, checking my mother's reactions to see how well I do.

She nods at each one of my statements, a little smile on her face. "Excellent! I'd say the same thing. What else? Why is she here?"

That's much harder for me to guess at. I have no idea why we're seeing so many of them. And why they're coming at night is a mystery as well. The woods back up to this complex with the barrier of a wide field between us and the trees. They seem to be coming from that direction because they all cluster at the rear fence. The rest seem to be coming from town because they wind up at the gate. This one is on the back side of the fence, which means it came from the woods.

"She's barefoot, but her feet aren't torn up enough for her to have been outside for all this time," I say, then think about what's beyond the woods. "That big subdivision, the one right before the farms start, the one with all the big houses? Maybe she came from there."

My mom nods and says, "That's what I was thinking. She's not that much different from the deaders I've been seeing lately. And you'll see the pattern when we get to the others."

She points to the clothes the deader is wearing and then waves a hand at a few others stuck to the fence a little farther down. "None of them are wearing discount clothes. Even the ones dressed for being outside are wearing good quality. And they're all wearing clothes suited for summer, which makes me agree with you that these people turned early. And, I agree with you on their condition. They're a mess and haven't been eating much in the way of fresh kills, but they aren't torn up by the elements. I think they were trapped inside somewhere, probably the houses in that subdivision. So, why is she here?"

As my mom speaks, it all sort of comes together for me. The amount of information we can get from a single deader is astounding, and I have a new appreciation for how thorough my mom is. I thought she was being a little obsessive, but she's kept us safe, always makes the right decision, and constantly seems one step ahead of what's happening. That's not the same kind of obsessive behavior as counting tiles on the floor or checking the locks over and over to no purpose. This is a different sort of obsessive, the good kind.

This is using everything around her to create a picture that is more complete than the one someone less observant would have. This is attention to detail. It's an edge.

"Okay, yeah. So if they were inside somewhere and now they are suddenly out, then something happened to let them out," I say, walking away to get a look at a few of the others. My mom says nothing and just lets me go and figure out what I can for myself.

The next three deaders don't just look like deaders to me now. They still don't resonate with me as human, which is a relief. Instead, they're puzzle pieces or clues to some mystery. And like the first deader, these are all barefoot, which is unusual. Shoes fall off, but running shoes and anything boot-like tends to stay on their feet pretty well, so long as they stay tied. And even if their shoes fall off, it's fairly common to see deaders with a ring of material banding their ankles or calves left over after the bottoms of their socks wear away. It's odd that there are no shoes or sock remains on any of these.

And like the first one, these deaders are all extremely withered, wearing light clothes and sporting wounds that signal how they died. Two of them are men and both of them have bare patches of bumpy nanite-grown skin on the backs of their heads. If I had to guess, I'd say both of them were shot or bludgeoned. The other is another woman, though this one is older. Like the girl, she's got a slit throat, but unlike the others, she's also sporting a pretty horrendous old bite wound. That one has scarred like a normal human's skin would. I think I'm starting to get a picture of their ends.

I don't want to look at them anymore. The picture is a sad one and I don't want to start thinking of them as humans, as they were when all this happened to them. I don't want to think of the woman with the bite being tended by others, succumbing, and then turning.

My mom is waiting for me, her eyes roaming the field and the woods beyond, ever watchful.

"Well?" she asks when I near.

"I think these people were trapped inside the houses at that subdivision and something has happened that is letting them out. Not a fire or anything because they aren't burned. Looters?"

She nods and says, "That's what I think too. Whoever is doing it either isn't confident enough to take them out or doesn't care that they wander afterward, which would mean they are pretty certain they can get out of the area once they're done searching the houses. That's looter behavior. And those are nice houses, so I'm guessing they aren't only scavenging after food and such."

I laugh and say, "Like jewelry is worth anything anymore. How stupid is that!"

She shrugs and says, "But it probably won't always be this way. Things change and this won't last forever. It could be a group so well organized that they're planning for the future. We'd need to watch out for any group like that coming this way."

The way she says that, I know our night watches are going to shift to cover the full period of darkness instead of ending around midnight. I sigh, but I'm also glad that I know what I might be looking for.

After this lesson, it's down to business. I know how to take out a deader with a sledge. The whole brain has to go and chopping off heads is just cruel because the head will stay alive for a long time. Not to mention the whole body twitching even without a head. I have no idea how long that goes on, but my mom apparently kept track of one for a while and says it's an unacceptably long time.

It's hard work and my arms feel like spaghetti by the time we're done dragging the last deader to the pile of them moldering in the field. I can see why my mom decided it's time for me to help. And, surprisingly, I'm okay with doing this kind of work. I suppose it's like anything else that's essentially disgusting. You can get used to anything.

Today – Breaching the Fortress of Death

As the two of us stare up at the apartment building, Sam starts in on his classic in-betweener stuff. As his snarls ratchet up, I get worried again. I'm going to need him so the kids who sent the note will know that I came at their request. I've got no more birds to give him, so we might be in trouble. Suddenly, he stops what he's doing, bangs his head against the car window, and then smacks himself with his bound hands again. I wait and eventually he points with his two hands toward the upper-right section of the building and says, "Da."

Before I get Sam out of the car, I gear up. When I'm done, it looks like I'm costumed for a very bad action movie. I have a cut down neck brace around my neck, the thick foam a hopeful defense against in-betweeners and deaders alike. My jacket is stifling in the heat, its double layers reinforced with bits of plastic trimmed away from containers to deflect bites. Shin guards liberated from a police cruiser by mom— somewhere and sometime on one of her runs—are matched by a cut-down pair of the same shielding my calves.

As for weapons, well, I've got an unsilenced handgun at my side as a last-ditch weapon, a rifle slung across my back in a terribly awkward position, and my crossbow hanging from my shoulder in a good position for bringing it up to bear and firing. A big homemade quiver full of bolts doesn't make the cut, which might be stupid, but I've got a whole slew of bolts jammed into loops I've sewn onto my "traveling pants," as my mother called them. The loops make me look like I've got wide thighs since they line the outer parts of each pant leg, but I love these pants.

Functionality completely rocks as the new fashion and weapons make the very best accessories.

To finish it off, I've got a variety of blades and a sharpened folding limb saw—meant for pruning trees—sheathed at my waist, along with a small sledgehammer for crushing heads. The sledge is heavy as hell, but it's the smallest one that'll do the job right. It takes a few whacks, but I can do it fairly quickly and that's the important part. Though I debate with myself over it, I grab one of my pokers as well. I need a weapon that will leave me out of arm's reach and a broom handle with a hedge-clipper blade attached works for me.

Sam watches me, managing to keep himself under control as I get ready. Nary a snarl comes from him and his jaws remain steadfastly unsnapping, but his hands twist against each other in their binding zip ties, so I know he's agitated. I'm just not sure if it's because he's worried for the kids or because he wants to eat me.

We reverse the process we used to get him inside the car, with a few modifications, and he's compliant to a fault. Once I have him at the other end of my dog-catching pole and in hand, he stumbles toward the door in rapid, unsteady steps. He's been cooped up inside the back of my little car and it seems to take him a while to get his legs back under him comfortably.

The stench hits me like a punch to the face when I get to the building's entrance. Sewage, rot, and old blood make a pungent scent so strong it should have a color, like in cartoons. Green and black clouds would be just right. Sam doesn't seem to notice it and leads me up the stairs faster than I'm comfortable with. I do my best to clear everything to the sides and in front of me, but there's no way to do that and still hang onto the dog-catcher.

It doesn't seem necessary once I realize someone—probably Sam when he was still Sam—has chained every door leading off the stairwell on each floor. Bright, shiny locks stand out inside the loops of old chain. He must have been so careful for so long. It's a lesson to me. Even someone with a PhD in Caution can wind up like Sam.

Two deaders loitering on the stairwell require us to stop so I can do my thing. It's very awkward because I've got Sam, but in the end, he actually helps me simply by being in front of me. They come for me, of course, but with Sam acting as interference, I manage to jab the blade on my poker through their faces enough times to get them to lie down for good. Once I finally push Sam past the mess, I bash them a few times with the sledgehammer just to be sure. Sam's mewls of distress at what I do makes me grit my teeth at the noise, but he calms down once I'm done. Well, he calms enough for me to push him upward and get him moving again.

At the fifth floor, Sam appears to lose it a little. There's no chain there, no lock, and the rim of the door is covered in bloody handprints and smears. This isn't good. Sam looks at the door and keens a terrible, sad noise.

"*Shh!*" I order in a whisper and shove him forward, up the stairs.

He pushes back for the first time. He has the advantage of being two steps above me and he's got about fifty pounds more body weight on top of that.

"Da! Da!" he urges, jabbing his purpling hands toward the door.

His zip ties are too tight and he's going to lose the ability to use his hands if I don't do something soon, but I'm not going to. His familiar face is my ticket inside, but I'm not at all sure what I'll do with him after. And given the blood all over the place out here, I'm thinking I might not need a ticket inside anymore.

"I know," I say calmly, even though I feel anything but calm. "I need both hands, so I'm going to secure you up there first. Okay?"

It takes him a second to understand me, but when he does, he rotates in his loop and eagerly takes the stairs up. He stops at the landing halfway between the floors and I push him into the corner, take the rope dangling from the handle of the dog-catcher, and tie him to the stout metal railing. He can't get close enough to the rope to untie it—even if he were able to untie a knot with his hands like that—and he can't get an angle sufficient to come down the stairs, but he can see the door and that should keep him quiet.

I don't waste time, even though the blood worries me enormously. It could just be Sam's, from when someone inside tended Sam when his "accident" occurred. Then again, it might not be. And those handprints aren't all his. Some of them are smaller, daintier…and newer than the others. I think I'm going to see something I really don't want to.

But I have to check, don't I? I do. I absolutely must.

At the door, I try to listen, but Sam's low keening sounds echo in the stairwell. It's disorienting, the noise seeming to come from both above and below us simultaneously. I turn to him and put my finger to my lips. He lowers the volume, but he doesn't stop. I don't think he can.

Sighing, I can only hope I don't get a hole in my chest for my trouble. I position myself behind the steel door and push it open slowly. I really hope that those kids have someone on watch who saw me pull up with Sam. I made sure he was plainly visible by stopping in the street for a moment. After all, the note asked me to come and get them and here I am.

"I'm here because of the note. Please don't shoot," I call out into the antechamber beyond.

No sounds return to me aside from a bit of echo from the stairs. I wait for a moment, then call again. And again, nothing. When I push open the door enough to slip inside, all I see is a lobby with a stained carpet, closed elevator doors, and two doors each on both the left and right. I don't know which one is the correct one for certain, but he looked right so I'm going for one of those.

Oh, and there are three more deaders. It's officially a party, I'm guessing.

One of them is quicker to get up than the others, so I loose a bolt at it. It's a good shot, right through the cheekbone. It stutter-steps a few times and then tips over. The other two are slower to rise, but they still give it the old college try.

In this smaller lobby space, I don't have a lot of space or time to maneuver, but the deaders are also in relatively bad shape. Bringing out my sledge, I whack the one on the ground and poke the closest standing one in the face. It takes a few minutes and definitely gets my blood pressure up, but in the end, there are three deaders who won't be getting up again.

Once I'm sure there aren't any more surprises, I look past all the blood and muck splattered around this floor's lobby and head for the doors. There's blood on the handle of the closest door, just like the door to the stairwell, only there's even more of it here.

"Shit," I say. "Shit, shit, *shit*." I'm too late, I'm guessing.

It seems unlikely that anyone hiding here would be discovered given how empty this place is, but what else can it be? In the back of my mind, I'm clinging to the hope that this is left over from someone tending Sam, or else dragging him out after what happened to him. Then again, I really have no idea how long ago Sam was given that note, or how long it might have taken him to get to me. I suppose anything could have happened. Anything at all.

The door is unlocked. I crack it open and nearly vomit at the smell that greets me. The stench of decay isn't enough to describe it. It's the stink that must have covered Europe when the plague killed whole villages and the bodies were left to rot. Only there's no wind to carry this stench away. It has been trapped inside this sealed apartment for who knows how long.

I should just walk away. I should just leave Sam where he is and go back to my lonely, but safe, warehouses. I should spare myself what I'm about to see. But I can't for some reason. I have to know.

Inside, I see just what I expected after all the clues on the doors and in the little lobby. The place has been wrecked, turned over, destroyed. I'd be tempted to say that it looks like it was looted, but the truth is bloodier than that. Someone or something has chased living things through the place, demolished impediments standing between them and their prey, and then proceeded to tear up the living things.

The ceilings, the walls, the sparse furnishings, even the bed sheets covering the windows are splattered with blood and gore. Underneath the dining table, chairs upended around it, is a round object about the size of someone's head. A small someone.

I know there were five kids here. As horrible as it is, I have to count heads. I have to see if there is even a slim possibility that anyone survived and is out there, waiting for rescue—or turned in-betweener.

Going through the apartment, with its high ceilings that might have once made the rooms feel decadently spacious, is an exercise in horror. Despite searching everything, I can find only three heads. Two are missing. One of the heads—this one on top of the bed like a discarded doll—is heartbreakingly small and has a single unmatted, copper-colored curl standing out from it. That almost undoes me.

I can't see any other place to look once I've checked the only bedroom. While the place is big, it has few rooms, sticking to the standard loft apartment dynamic of much space in the main room and few rooms outside of that. I cover the head on the bed with a towel still hanging over the rack in the bathroom, which smells revolting since they've been using buckets for a toilet and who knows how often they emptied them.

My deep breath sounds loud in the room now that I can't hear Sam, and I say to the little lump on the bed, "I'm sorry I didn't get here in time. So very sorry."

That's when I hear a shuffling noise behind me. I turn quickly and bring up the crossbow, a reaction now as instinctive as breathing. There's nothing there except a wall. Then I see the big grating where the air filter in a central air system goes. My heart lifts.

"Are you there? If you are, I'm Emily. I got your note. I came for you," I say, trying to keep my voice calm, but knowing that the noise might well be nothing more than a rat seeking a noisome meal.

Nothing comes back to me. Rat, for sure. I lower the crossbow, my heart taking a rapid trip back downward into despair.

"Are you really alive?" asks a small voice, young, female, and terribly afraid.

I smile at the grate and say, "I am! And you must be too."

One Year Ago - You Can't Plan for Everything

My mom is sick, as in *really* sick. We've been doing well and I thought staying away from people would mean that we wouldn't catch anything. I thought that because my mom said that was so, but now she's the one who is sick.

"Baby girl, the water…you'll have to boil it better, strain it first," she says between wretches.

She's leaking from both ends and so dehydrated she's shriveling. I nod and toss the water I have onto the cement as I go. She needs more and if I have to re-boil it, I'll need to hurry. If she gets any more dehydrated I may not be able to get her back.

The barrels are full. We've had so much rain that it cascades from the downspouts in waterfalls and we've got a barrel or four under each one. Set up on pallets and concrete blocks, their heights are staggered so that I'll get a continuous flow from one barrel to the next. I fill up a bucket and inspect it. It looks like water to me, but she's probably right. Something bad lurks inside the innocent-looking liquid.

I don't have sand or anything like that to strain it with, but there's a boat-load of stuff I can rig together—fish filters, air filters, gravel from the decorative beds at the front of the complex, cotton batting—so I do, using charcoal filters for now. We haven't been great about boiling it, mostly just doing it in batches and letting it set until we need it, but clearly we've got something nasty somewhere.

I'm not sick, but it's only a matter of time if the water is the source of our problem. I boil up a smaller batch than we have been, using a smaller pot and letting it come to a full rolling boil. Five minutes of that, then I take the pot off. Rather than pour it into containers—which might have been the source of the problem for all I know—I bring the whole pot over and set it on the concrete to cool.

"I've got more, Mom. Just hang on," I say, going for a soothing tone, like she used to do for me. She's pulled into a fetal position on the concrete and jerking with spasms. She twists like she needs to rise, but her bowels let go before she can and a stinking stream of brown water comes out of her. That's disgusting, but it's also very bad. It's just colored water now.

"So sorry," she groans and then folds into herself even tighter.

I clean up the mess as best I can, tossing my gloves afterward. I'm running low on them and have no idea what I'll do after I use the last of them. Maybe I can wash them somehow. When I lean over to wipe her sweating face, she opens her eyes and jerks backward at the sight of my bare hands.

"No, don't touch me. Be safe," she says weakly. I drop the cloth on the floor and she takes it to wipe her face. She's in her respite stage. After she has a bout of puking and crapping, she feels better for a few minutes before it starts again.

"What do I do, Mom?" I ask.

"Nothing," she answers. "No. Something." She turns her head and points with her eyes toward the other end of the warehouse.

"No," I say, turning the word into an absolute refusal.

"Yes," she whispers, and closes her eyes.

I look at the dark corner and see the shadows of the chain link even from where I am. It's one of the reasons we chose to stay here after we had to leave the lawyer's office where we hid out for a while. Aside from the fact that there was a warehouse of food that had barely been touched—these distribution hubs aren't usually so close to towns and this was a smaller one—it had more bonuses than I can count. There were the wide views, the flat landscape, the lack of traffic or reasons for traffic, the fence—and then that chain link-surrounded room. A sort of safe room for us if we needed it.

If the place ever *did* get overrun, we had a floor-to-ceiling box of sturdy chain link that we could lock ourselves into and still shoot out of. Once a holding section for the smaller, higher value goods like anti-aging creams and perfume, we emptied it and filled it with food and necessities for a long stay. At first, we slept in there every night, finally feeling like there was enough between us and the deaders to sleep deeply.

Now, we prefer the office for its metal-meshed window and limited approaches.

That chain link room has another benefit. You can lock someone inside it. Someone sick who might die.

"Please, no," I plead.

It's a step too far, locking her up. It's like an admission that I'll be alone and she's going to become one of them. She's more than likely infected. She's fought too many of them, bathed in too much of their fluids, for her not to be. If she dies…well.

"Yes," she repeats, and tries to get to her feet.

*****

Inside the cage—behind the warehoused rows of boxed-up Asian sauces, bags of tortilla flour, and packaged Indian food—she seems to feel better. Maybe because from her point of view, she's got one less worry if the worst happens. When I bring her another fresh pot of water, she rallies enough to talk to me.

"I think this is dysentery," she says. "Classic, huh?" She almost laughs. Almost.

"What can I do for it?" I ask.

"Honestly, without a computer and the internet, I wouldn't know. Maybe antibiotics?"

"Where?" I ask.

She clutches her stomach as another cramp takes her on. When she looks up, a fresh coat of shiny sweat bathes her face in the light of the lantern. I can see that she's trying to decide if she should tell me something or if it would be safer just to let the disease take its course.

"If you don't tell me, I'll go looking on my own. You can't leave me here alone!" I say, my voice rising at the end. It's manipulative, I know, but leaving me alone is what she fears more than death, I think. She's my mom.

"Vet hospital down the road might have some," she says. For her to actually say that means she's feeling bad enough that she's willing to endure risk to me to make it go away. That, or my little jab worked on her maternal instincts and she'd rather I at least have a destination in mind.

"You said to stay away from hospitals," I say.

She shakes her head and says, "Not now so much and not one for animals. It might be looted and not have anything anyway. I've been meaning to go there and check it, but time sort of slipped away from me. This area has been empty so far, so it should be safe. Just don't let anyone see you. People are worse than deaders."

Words seem to fail her then as the cramps rise in intensity. She starts panting she's in such pain. I've never seen a person lose this much of themselves. When I was sick, I remember seeing my mother's alarm during the bad period when chemo was taking its toll on me.

Now our positions are reversed. She's wasting away. I'm not sure if it's dehydration, but she's shrinking into herself. I've got to get her set up with water for drinking, buckets of water for washing herself, and some of the broth from the endless cans of it in the warehouse.

And then, I'm guessing I'm going on a trip.

Today - Company

Veronica is her name, the same Veronica who wrote the note with her young-girl loops and circles. She's been inside the little closet for days with a toddler, a little boy. This must be the Jon from her note and he's adorable. He's far too quiet for a kid as little as he is, and he doesn't smile, but I suppose that's understandable. Given his age, he must have been only a tiny baby when the world went to hades, if he was even born before it happened.

When Veronica comes out, leading Jon by the hand, her face crumples at the sight of the apartment. She cries fresh tears into the tracks on her dirty face when she spots the towel-covered lump on the bed.

"Penny," she whispers.

I nod, thinking that I'm glad I covered it up. There are no flies in here, which is amazing to me, but the sight is bad enough, even without the head showing.

"You've been in there the whole time?" I ask. "Why didn't you come out and leave the apartment?" I bend and look into the dark little room. Someone pulled the duct away and there is, at most, six feet of space next to the air conditioning equipment. A door on the other side of the closet-like room has been nailed shut from the inside. There's a nearly empty jug of water, a bucket that smells bad and a small nest of blankets tucked in the open space. It's one of those machinery spaces you see in apartments sometimes, places where the management can get to do maintenance, but the tenants don't have access to. Except, of course, if you're smart like these guys were and tear out the duct. Whoever set this up meant it to be a hiding place of last resort.

When I turn around and get to my feet, she's examining me, more than a little wary of strangers. Which is exactly as it should be.

Veronica averts her eyes when I catch her looking and says, "Sam had the keys to all the other places somewhere, but I don't know where and I was afraid to go outside. I…I was just afraid."

"You wrote the note. How did you get Sam to take it to me?" I ask as I lead her and the boy into the smelly, but unbloodied, bathroom. I'm genuinely curious about this. If there is some way to keep in-betweeners at least somewhat tame, as Sam is, then I want to know about it.

At the mention of Sam's name, her face crumples again and I pat her back as she cries. She's been through something horrific and I have patience. My other PhD.

After she and the little boy drink their fill from a bucket of water, she quickly strips Jon down and washes him from another bucket on the counter, this one containing grayish-looking water. He's filthy and he's had more than one accident in his pants by the look of things. She seems better while she's doing this bit of domestic business, like maybe doing practical things can distract her from all the rest. Still, she doesn't speak for a moment.

The water must be cold, because Jon gives out a single peep of distress when she touches him with the cloth, but he lapses back into silence almost immediately.

"Sam told us about you. He watched you for a while, tried to decide if it might be safe to contact you. The food in this area is running out. We needed to find someplace where the kids can get some fresh air and sun," she says matter-of-factly. She waves her cloth-filled hand over Jon's pale torso and I see what she means. He's as white as I've ever seen any human, yet he has dark hair and brown eyes.

I nod and say nothing.

She darts a look up at me from under her brow, but looks away when she meets my eyes. "He told us about you. Before he...uh...changed, I mean."

"Of course," I answer. "Why didn't you contact me?"

"Sam was going to, but then..." The words trail off. She doesn't have to explain.

"But how did you get him to come to me afterwards?" Referring to his demise with the bland "afterwards" seems safer to me, less likely to cause more tears and delay.

She's finished washing the boy, who stands naked and shivering on the counter, perfectly uncomplaining. It's summer outside, but inside this bathroom, with the only window facing north, it's cooler and the water has taken all his heat away. He's skinny. Very skinny. She's right—they do need food, and badly.

Inside my pocket is a packet of candy. There are pallets of the stuff at the warehouse and these fruity gels are fortified with vitamins. I pull out the package and open it. The smell is almost lost in the fecal stench, but these two must smell it. Both of their heads whip around and their eyes focus on the plastic pouch. I look to Veronica for permission and she nods, so I hand one of the jellied candies to Jon. He snatches it from my fingers and puts it into his mouth so fast he reminds me of a wild animal.

I hold the package out to Veronica. I can see she's tempted, but she says, "No. Jon needs it." Then she pauses, looking at the brightly colored plastic bag, and asks, "Do you have more? I mean, where you live?"

I nod and say, "Enough for all of us."

Eleven Months Ago - I'll Stay With You

I can hear her shuffling around inside the cage, but I can't see her anymore. That's good because I don't think I can bear much more of that. She has nothing in there. Nothing to eat and nothing to rebuild herself with. She's not just rotting, she's desiccating. Even so, she's still an in-betweener and dangerous beyond belief.

The corrugated metal and pallet structure I've constructed around her cage blocks the view, but not the sounds. I come here and listen every day, waiting for the day when her grunts and warbles go silent, waiting for the day she goes full-on deader and I can be sure she's really gone. Now, listening is a torment because I wonder how much of my mother is trapped inside that brain, a brain so cooked by fever that when she died she had no idea who I was.

But she wasn't gone long at all. Just two minutes of silence and then I heard her suck in a breath, deep and ragged. That's not long. People came back from that before the nanites were updated and lived normal lives as far as I know. The brains of the veggie-people were deprived of blood and oxygen for much longer. But the fever in her brain had been at a low simmer for days before she finally, mercifully, died.

I feel so bad about all of this, about her being in that cage, about her dying, about not being able to save her. If anyone should have died, it should have been me. My time was years ago, yet I'm still here and taking up space. My mom was healthy, strong...a contributor to this world.

And even more than that, she has that program she's been working on that might be able to help with the nanites. We sort of gave up on the idea of being able to get it to anyone, but there was always a chance. When she died, that chance died with her. And I'm still here, useless and alone.

And afraid. I'm so afraid I can barely function. I'm not even sure I want to go on like this. Are people even capable of surviving when there is no other living thing around them? Well, I suppose I have the birds. That's something.

I sigh and, in response, a loud, rattling bang comes from the cage. Her snarls aren't particularly loud, but they *are* mean and hungry. She's getting more desperate, but I don't think it's really her inside that body. I think that's her nanites working on her instincts for food. I think, but I don't know.

"I love you, Mom," I whisper, so quietly it's more breath than words, and listen to the banging that travels back to me.

When she quiets again, I get to my feet as quietly as I can. Even the smallest noise will get her going again. I can't kill her, though I know I should, and it's not just because she told me not to. She thought her in-betweener ways would stop anyone who might come here looking for spoils, or at least give me warning so I could escape. Even when near death, she was working to keep me safe.

Creeping out of the warehouse, I have to shield my eyes from the bright light of the day. It's high summer, hot and still, like the world has been set to simmer on a celestial stove. I'm late for work and the day isn't going to get any cooler, so there's no point in putting it off.

My gear is piled here by the door, so I start strapping on my tools. Hammers, knives, my crossbow and trusty sledge. It's like armor and with every bit that goes onto my body, I feel a little more detached from the remains of my mother in the cage. I feel less overwhelmingly sad.

I'm not sure what that means, but I don't think it's healthy. Mostly because I think it means that I'm beginning to look forward to my work each day. This is not the kind of work anyone is supposed to be pleased to do.

The birds look at me as I make my way to the back fence, my bag of deader restraints bumping against my leg as I go. I wave up at them and say, "Hey." One of the pigeons jerks its head and cocks it so that it can get a better look at me. I don't think that one likes me too much.

There are at least ten deaders along the stretch of fence in the back and none of them look very lively today. The first one in my line was probably a girl near my age, maybe a little older. It's hard to tell because her face is gray and green, but she's wearing a very cool set of bracelets on her wrists. They're the kind I used to make with my mom out of hemp and beads. I used to love doing that.

"So, Sunshine, wanna tell me where you live so I can go get your craft supplies? I *love* your bracelets," I say brightly as I feed a loop of wire through one of the links so I can put it around her neck. As the wire brushes her, she lifts her face, the ragged mess that remains of her tongue darting out to get a taste of it. Her fingers wrap around the links near my face.

She doesn't answer me, but that's okay. I wouldn't leave to go get craft stuff anyway, but it's a good conversation opener. "Playing hard to get, eh?" I quip and drop the loop of wire around her head. As I pull it tight and loop the length of pipe through so that she can't leave the fence, she stumbles a little and winds up hanging by her neck for a moment.

There's definitely more pep in her movements as she regains her feet. She must realize what I am and that I'm food. Her ragged teeth clamp onto the links and her nostrils flare as she breathes me in.

I tap her nose with a gloved fingertip, making her jerk against the fence and say, "That's okay. We've got all day. I'm sure you'll warm up to me eventually."

Yes, work is a good way to forget my troubles.

Today - Sam

With Jon dressed again in halfway-clean clothes taken from a clothesline strung across the bathroom, Veronica has nothing to occupy her eyes and hands, so she turns to me.

"Are you really going to take us with you?" she asks.

"I am. But we should go soon in case anyone saw me driving around earlier," I answer, squeezing past her to the bathroom window so I can peek out and look for movement. There's none. There's only this beautiful day with its high, clear, and blue sky.

She pulls down a few more pieces of miniature clothing from the line and says, "What should I bring?"

"Clothes," I answer quickly. "That's pretty much the only thing I don't have a lot of. I hope you like foreign food."

"Huh?" she asks, confused.

"Forget it. I'm just nervous and talking stupid," I answer and wave my stupidity away. These two are starving. They'll like anything that's even remotely edible. I have no idea how to talk to people anymore. I haven't been around anyone in at least a year that hasn't been dead at least once.

Plus, I'm more than nervous. I'm terrified. Until I get back inside the safe confines of my fences, I'm not going to feel safe. And this place is not safe at all.

While she pulls things off the clothesline strung across the bathroom, I remember the state of the rest of the apartment, and what is likely covering anything not in a drawer or closet. When she reaches for the bathroom door, I put my hand on her wrist and say, "No. Just tell me where stuff is and I'll get it. And a bag for it."

Her hand falls from the knob and she nods. After she tells me what to look for, I go back out into the slaughterhouse that is their home and put what I can find—what is packable and not covered in gore—into a big backpack and return, helping her to hoist it onto her back. I find the baby carrier where she said it would be and bring that back as well. Jon is really too big for it, but she stuffs him into it all the same. He protests as his thighs get pinched by the too-narrow openings, but once inside, he goes silent again.

With Jon balanced on her front and the backpack on her back, her load isn't too heavy for her to carry. I need my hands free, ready to use weapons. We've been in here a while and the car is parked right outside like a big, flashing blue light announcing our location to anyone who saw me driving earlier.

"Cover his eyes while we go. Just keep your eyes straight ahead. Okay?"

Veronica nods, swallows loudly, and slips her hand over Jon's face. He doesn't squirm or try to pull her hand away, which is inexpressibly sad, but also useful. We walk through the bedroom and into the large main room. It's a long way to walk through so much carnage, particularly when that includes bits and pieces of people she may have loved.

I don't pause. I just grab her elbow and say, "Close your eyes if you want." I don't wait for her to hesitate, I just pull her behind me. We make it a few steps before she stops suddenly, yanking me backward. I know she must have looked and is now seeing what I'd hoped she wouldn't.

Veronica is staring at the head under the dining table, her mouth open and her hand shaking over Jon's eyes. I should have covered it when I left the bathroom to grab the clothes. I reach out and push her fingers back together so that Jon won't see, hissing, "Get a grip! He can't see this!"

Her eyes dart to my face and then back to the head. She can't stop looking. I grab a blood-soaked blanket off the couch and toss it under the table so that it covers the head. The other head, thank goodness, is on the other side of the couch where she can't see it.

"Piper," she whispers.

"I'm sorry about her. Truly. But it's over for her. She's not in pain and she can't feel that. She's gone for good."

"My fault," she says, softly. Her eyes get watery, but no tears fall. I think she needs sleep and food and water before her body is going to be fit for a truly good cry. Her lips are so chapped they're almost white.

I shake my head. "No, this isn't your fault. This isn't your doing any more than anything in this world is."

She looks at the blanket-covered lump and says, "Oh yes. Yes, it can be." She says this with such certainty, in such a low and adult voice, that I get a chill.

"We should go. You can tell me later. After we get there and you two get some food and rest, you can tell me everything," I say and take her elbow again. At the door, I say, "And I've got Sam with me, so you can see him again."

At my words, she freezes in place like she's just been transformed into one of the slender pillars holding up the ceiling in this big room.

"Here?" she asks, her voice a fearful squeak.

"Yes," I confirm, confused. "He brought me the note."

"You didn't kill him?"

"No, why would I? He's been helpful, in his own way. I thought...I thought you might like to see him again, so you could be sure I was one of the good guys."

Veronica shrinks back from me, glancing at the door behind me, at the unbolted lock. She looks like she's about to take off for the torn-out air duct again and get back into her closet.

"What? You want me to take him away first?" I ask, then look at Jon. "You don't want Jon to see him like that. I get it. We can get past so that Jon won't see. I promise."

She's shaking her head and backing up. She's about to step into a pile of stuff that was once inside someone else's body, so I say, "Stop." I glance down behind her, so she knows what

I'm saying. She freezes again, blanching even more. She looks like she's going to faint for a second, but it passes.

"You don't understand," she begins. There's a bitter sort of smile on her face that turns into an angry grimace. "Sam did this."

I look around the room, then think back to the blood on his hands and his shirt, the stains streaking his jeans a darker blue. "Oh, crap."

She nods at my words, then jerks her head toward the lump under the table. "Sam, when he died, was right by the door. It was an accident. I was on watch and I heard noises. I didn't know he'd gone out. I just saw a shape coming in the door and…"

I can picture exactly what she's saying. In this world, fear makes a person more likely to pull the trigger because those who don't pull it fast enough probably aren't capable of pulling a trigger at all. Those who can't shoot without thinking too much about it are dead or walking around dead.

"I can see that happening," I say, truthfully.

"I dragged him out of the door, super quickly, because…well…you know. When he came back, he was like the others, but after a while, he quieted down. Then he started trying to talk. You've heard him?" she asks.

"I have. That's how he got my attention. It's why I didn't kill him again."

"It took a few days to figure out that he could understand more than he could say and we shoved birds through the mail slot for him. That kept him calm." She points with her eyes toward the glass door leading to their balcony. There are simple box traps all over it I hadn't noticed before.

"It was Jeremy who said we should try to send him for you. He'd been watching you for so long and we were just about ready to go and meet you, maybe get some transportation somehow out to you. Jeremy thought Sam might remember who you were. He did, so I wrote the note and put it through the slot. I couldn't be sure he understood, but I saw him pick up the note. With him between the door to the stairs and us, there was no way we could leave anyway. And we had no food left at all by then, so we had nothing left to lose by giving him the note."

She stops and looks at the lump again.

"What happened, Veronica?" I ask.

"Piper was special. You know what I mean? Not as bad off as some, but she had difficulties."

I have no clue what she's saying, so I shake my head.

"Down syndrome. Not bad, but definitely there," she finally says.

"Ah, okay." I have no idea what bearing that has on anything, but I don't want her to stop now. If Sam did this, I'm going to have to make a decision really soon and I'd like to know why I'm making it. He just saved two lives...but he took three. Using the cold rules of survival-based calculations, he is on the losing side of my equation. I had thought maybe he might be useful, an in-betweener who can walk around freely might be a good way to find out if there are more people in our vicinity.

"When I left the room to take care of Jon—he was very sick, and we didn't want the other kids to get what he had—Piper opened the door for him. Just like that."

I can see it now. Sam is there, but not all there. I've seen him go from the way he is now, more or less in control, to full-on in-betweener quickly. I've also seen him come back from it, banging his head in some terrible grief. He must have been a good man before. And now I know the reason for that grief. It wasn't for himself, for his situation. It was for these children.

"What do you want me to do about him?" I ask. She has the right to make this decision for herself. She's the aggrieved party here.

"I don't want him to hurt anyone anymore. I don't want him to suffer anymore," Veronica answers without hesitation.

Her hand is cold in mine when I take it and draw her toward the door again. "He's secure. I'll get you past him and then I'll take care of it."

When I open the stairwell door, Sam becomes agitated, straining at the end of his leash on the landing and trying to see. His noises are more grunt than speech, but I know what he's asking. Rather than answer, I lead Veronica and Jon out of the foyer and urge them toward the stairs going down. She almost makes it without looking, but at the last second, she stops and looks up.

I can see her eyes take in his leash, his purple zip-tied hands, the bits of gore that still cover him from his breakfast of birds. Her face crumples and she chokes out a sob. I look at Sam and see his face is almost a mirror of hers, only a cruder and more uncomplicated version of it. That makes it all the more heartbreaking and I feel the sting of sadness behind my cheeks. Tears, I don't have time for now, but the sting is worse because of it.

He grunts, then hums a sort of concentrated tone as he tries to find his voice. Finally, he forces out two words. "Lub. Zahry."

I know what those words mean right away.

Love. Sorry.

That does Veronica in and she hugs Jon to her as she sobs. Rather than freezing her in place, his words seem to free her and she takes the stairs rapidly downward and away from us.

"Wait on the second floor," I call in a harsh whisper after her. I hope she's smart enough not to go outside if she didn't hear me.

Sam is agitated again, hitting his head and keening softly. I could just leave him there. He's tied up and that railing is strong. There's no way he could free himself. Eventually, like my mom, he'd slow down and go deader, then after a time, truly die.

It's almost as if he hears my thoughts because he stops hitting himself and looks at me, fresh blood leaking from his nose in bright crimson drops. He shakes his head, then raises his chin and slides his hands across his neck in the sign for cutting off a head.

He's done his job and he is suffering. I can see that. Don't I owe him a clean death?

I bring up the crossbow and say, "Stand still. I'll try to be quick."

He doesn't try to talk anymore, but he pulls the wire of the dog-catcher's loop down a little, exposing his neck to me at a better angle, and then lifts his chin. There's no hesitation in his movements at all. After blinking away the tears blurring my vision, I let the bolt go after an extra careful sighting. It drives home perfectly at the exact center of his neck. His legs loosen under him and he flops to the ground as if all his bones were suddenly gone.

He jerks horribly after a second of unnatural stillness, his nanites going into their expected overdrive and his body in no way under control. I race up the stairs because there's no time to spare, and decide against using the saw. He doesn't need to suffer through that. His eyes are wide and rolling, focusing on me in pure confusion when they are drawn to my movement.

I pull out the sledge and set to work.

*****

I take the time to wipe myself off with another towel left in the bathroom. On my way back out, I spot the bookcases. They're full of hard- and soft-cover books. Hundreds of them. If I hadn't been so overwhelmed by the condition of the apartment, I would have noticed them before. I told Veronica I have all we need at my complex, but that's not strictly true. I have a few trashy books and a lot of hours in the day with not much to fill them.

I grab the less bloody of the two pillowcases off the bed, careful to avoid the towel-covered head, and fill it with as many paperback books as it will hold. It's heavy, but worth it.

I don't look at Sam as I leave, but I can't help getting a glimpse of his feet hanging over the edge of the landing, the man inside finally gone to his rest.

"Goodbye, Sam. Thank you," I say, and take to the stairs.

Six Months Ago - Before I Lay Me Down to Sleep

"**M**om, can you hear me?" I ask from my spot on the concrete a few feet from the barrier.

I push away my empty bowl and pull my legs in so I can sit cross-legged. I like to spend time here. It may seem creepy, but I come here to eat my main meal of the day. We always did that together before she died. Today is my day for splurging on food, so I had one of the packets of instant miso soup, a pouch of the Indian chickpea stuff—my mom called them Indian MREs—and rice.

This hub must have serviced a whole lot of international grocery stores and at least some quick-marts. The amount of candy and weird food is staggering.

Even though there is still plenty of it in the warehouse, the levels are lowering and some of my favorite things are gone. As much as I would like to just eat whatever I want to and ignore the realities, I can't. So, I've begun to ration my food more carefully. I give myself one day a week to eat my fill, but the rest of the time, I eat only what I think I need.

It's hard to guess what's right though. I measure my guesses based on whether or not I shrink. If I do, then I increase the amount I eat. If I start to gain some girth, I lower it. It's all a guessing game at this point.

"Mom, do you remember what the brown sauce in the jars is called? I can't remember and the label isn't in English," I say.

Hardly anything comes back to me, just that shushing sound.

"Today's my birthday. I'm officially an adult," I say after a minute of listening to the sound of cloth or something brushing the concrete. She's moving, but how much?

She's been a lot quieter for the past few weeks. When I look at my chart, the one she outlined on the back of a big piece of cardboard before she got too sick, I see the trend is inexorably downward. Her responses have grown progressively less violent and less vocal.

There's the *tink tink* sound of something small moving along the chain link and I know it's her ring. Her hand. The only vocalization is a sort of raspy noise, like loud breathing that's also shallow and unfulfilling to the lungs. If she even has much in the way of lungs anymore.

"Mom, I'm so lonely," I say.

More rasping, more of that same weak agitation.

"I'm thinking that...that I can't do this much longer. It's too much alone time." I laugh as a thought comes to me. "Do you remember when I was so sick the first time, how I used to beg you to take me home so people would leave me alone?"

More tinking noises and the sliding shuffle of dry flesh against concrete.

"I got my wish, didn't I?" I ask the corrugated metal in front of me.

I listen for a little while, then get up and stand against the metal, which is as close as I can get to her. I know that she wanted to stay alive for me and I know she tried as hard as she could. And I also know that she asked me to do this, to measure and monitor her like this, so that I could know how long this whole bad episode might last.

She wanted me to be able to make good decisions about when to go and try to find other people, if ever. And she wanted to be a deterrent to whoever might come into this warehouse. My own private in-betweener—then deader—to keep others away.

But it's so hard. She couldn't have known how hard it would be for me to be so entirely alone.

"Mom," I say again, my mouth close to the metal so I can be sure my words go through it. "I miss you. I love you."

I hear the *tink tink* again of her ring and look at my pinkie where its mate resides. Our birthstones set into the sign for infinity. One in each side of the sign. Her and me, together forever.

Mine only fits on my pinkie now, though when she gave it to me it was almost too big for any of my fingers. Right before my first brain surgery, she opened the box and told me what the rings and the infinity symbol meant. Together forever, our hearts and souls entwined no matter what.

Back then, we didn't know there would be a nanite miracle to save my life someday. All we knew was that I was going to have my skull sawed open and chunks of my brain taken out along with as much of the tumor as could be teased out. We didn't even know if I would wake up again. When she put that ring on my finger and then put on her own, we'd clasped our hands together, fingers entwined.

The rings made that tinking sound then too.

I tap my pinkie against the metal, adding my *tink tink* to hers, then wait. I hear the rasping and I want to read into it, to imagine some meaning behind her shuffles and noises, but I know there isn't.

Then I hear it.

Tink tink.

Today - Bumpity-Bump

The trip back is going smoothly, except that Jon appears to be getting car-sick and Veronica looks a little green as well. If neither of them has been in a car since this happened then it's understandable, but the smell of my drive over with Sam in the back is still bad enough without adding puke to the mix.

"If you're going to hurl, try to do it out the window," I say, keeping my eyes on the road and the deaders drawn by the disturbance my car creates in their endlessly boring afterlives.

"I'm not hanging Jon out of the window," she snaps back, then swallows hard and looks forward again. Definitely greenish.

"If you keep your eyes forward it isn't so bad. Don't look to the sides." I risk a glance over and see that Jon's eyes are darting everywhere. He's not had this much new visual input in his life, I'd bet. "Jon, can you do that? Just look ahead?"

He seems to understand me because he faces forward, but when I glance back, he's looking every which way again. I sigh.

I can almost feel it coming, and sure enough, he spews a stream of high-powered bile and fruit-gel-colored slime straight at the windshield.

He seems surprised by it, then his face screws up and he starts to cry. It's quiet, but intense, the way a child who knows sound is the enemy would cry.

"Crap!" I say, and reach under the seat for the little towel I use to wipe off the windows.

When my eyes leave the road, which is entirely clear of other than the normal debris, Veronica shouts, "There's one coming!"

I look back up and have just enough time to think, *How much like a freaking movie is this?*

An in-betweener in bad shape is making a beeline for us in the street and there's no way I'm going to get past him without hitting him. This is a fairly narrow, one-way street and it's lined with parked cars on both sides. I shout, "Hold on!" and swerve left, then remember the rolled-down window on her side of the car and spin the wheel the other way so we'll take the hit on my side.

Only, I've admitted before that I'm a terrible driver and this is a terrible idea.

I hit him firmly on my half of the bumper, but instead of going under or bouncing off, he slams into the hood hard enough for me to hear the metal buckle under the impact. The airbags pop out and Veronica makes a muffled squeal as Jon is thrust against her face.

Then I make matters very much worse by hitting a parked car and crunching the other half of my front bumper. We jolt to a stop in a squeal of tires and the *whoosh* of deflating airbags.

"Crap on a stick!" I say and punch at the airbag. My language, however bad it is today, is simply not enough to describe how much this situation sucks. The in-betweener flew off of the car and is somewhere in front of it, banging and making a racket.

I can't have him making even more noise than my wreck just made. A wreck happens, is loud, and is then over, making it hard to pin down where the noise came from. An in-betweener having a meltdown, on the other hand, is sure to draw a crowd.

"Stay put!" I order the two crying kids in the seat next to me. I spare a single glance and see that both of them are upright and have open eyes, but their faces are both spattered with blood. I can only hope it's not serious.

Two fast, deep breaths, then I open the door and leap from the car. I slam the door closed as soon as I'm clear and pull out my sledge at the same time. I've got no time for this and can only hope he's down.

When I step around the front of the car—wary and ready for anything—he sort of lunges in my direction from his place under the crumpled front end. He's half under it and his back is pressed against the car I hit. I came within a foot of squishing him like a bug between the two cars, but the lucky bastard fits nicely in the wedge of space the angle of impact allows.

I don't hesitate and give him time to work his way out. I swing my sledge like I'm driving home a railroad tie over his

ANN CHRISTY

reaching hands and toward his head. I've got the front of the car between us, so my angle is off and the sledge just sort of swipes down the side of his head and face, bones crunching as it does. Not enough.

Clambering up onto the hood, I get as close as I dare and get ready to bring it down again. His hands are still reaching and he manages to get his ragged nails into my knee and clamp down like a vice. I bring the sledge down on his wrist and it crunches like old twigs. The fingers loosen and he flings the arm, now possessing an extra joint, in my direction harmlessly.

When I swing the sledge this time, my center of balance shifts during the swing—the total amateur move of someone without knowledge of basic physics, which I do have, so it's unforgivable. I slide right down the hood and into his space, one foot on his shoulder and the other braced against the car I hit. The way we're positioned is almost pornographic except that the place his face is close to is unarmored and within range of his teeth.

I straighten my legs with a panicked jerk and he clamps his mouth around my shin. The sound of teeth meeting the hard plastic of my shin guards replaces his horrible screeching. I've got a better angle now and the sledge does its work, his teeth clamping down hard with the first blow and then falling away from my body. I hit him at least a half a dozen times, his head nothing more than a pulpy bulge of red atop his neck by the time I stop.

The sound of crying reaches my ears over my breathless gasps and my sledge *thunks* against the hood. My arms are so tired they're shaking. Sledgehammers aren't meant for awkward, fast swinging, but rather for careful and steady strikes.

I get down from the hood and realize I'm covered head to toe in blood and bits of in-betweener brain. Through the window, Veronica looks at me in horror as she holds Jon in her lap facing away from me. Fluttering from a lamppost above the car I hit is a ragged banner announcing a forthcoming civic event. I'm pretty sure all events have been cancelled, so they won't miss the banner. I climb up on that car, rip the banner down, and use it to wipe off as much gore as I can. I don't want this on me and I don't want Jon to see it.

Veronica keeps half an eye on me while she uses Jon's shirt to clean them both up. I'm still stained red, but the chunks and goop are gone, so I jump down and get back into the car, hoping against reason that it will still start. The front of my car looks like an accordion. This wreck is a lot worse than a fender bender. I still have a working car because it's electric and small enough for me to take care of. That also means it isn't up to major impacts caused be once-dead cannibals and bad teen drivers.

I don't say anything when I get in. I close my eyes for a moment, make a wish, and turn the key. Nothing whatsoever happens. Nothing.

"Dammit," I say and lean my head on the steering wheel and its deflated air bag. Without looking up, I ask, "How bad are you hurt?"

When Veronica doesn't answer, I open one eye and look at her. She's got a goose-egg coming up on her forehead where the airbag knocked their heads together, but the blood doesn't appear to be coming from her. She dabs at Jon's forehead and says, "Not bad. Jon's head is cut, though. I might need to close it somehow."

"We're about eight miles from where I live. We're going to have to hoof it. Can you do that? Can he?"

She blots his forehead again and smiles at him in that fake way parents do when their child is in pain. Finally, she looks at me and answers. "We'll have to."

There are a good half-dozen deaders making their way toward us, so there's more work to do before we can safely leave. On foot, we'll be able to distance ourselves from this source of noise. We'll walk quietly and stay out of sight. We'll watch and avoid. But for now, I've got more bolts to loose and more heads to smash.

I just know my shoulders are going to be hurting tonight.

One Month Ago - Forever

It's summer again and it's been a year since she died. A full year of first watching and listening, and then just listening. That's long enough. I can't take even one more day of it. One more day of not knowing what's going on behind the wall of metal and wood and I know I'll go completely insane.

I heft the claw hammer and start pulling nails. I'm so naturally frugal now that, even without thinking too much, I remove the nails carefully, trying to keep them straight in case I need them again. This is more noise than I've made near the cage in a long time. I'd expect to hear more agitation, more movement, but all I hear is a soft whisper of sound between each tug on a nail.

When the last nail pops out, I suck in a deep breath and get ready for what I might see. I know I'm not ready, because all I can think is that I'll see my mom again. But it's not my mom. I have to remember that.

"Get a grip," I whisper, then wiggle the piece of corrugated metal away from its mates. This one is my doorway piece, with no wood behind it. Every other piece of the metal has a messy construction of pallet boards keeping it upright and firmly in place.

I put the metal aside and then stand, not turning around and with my back to the opening in full view of the cage. If she's still capable of moving, and if she has eyes, she can see me. If she has any of her senses intact, she should react.

There's only a faint leathery swish and then that fades too.

I turn around and finally see what has become of my mother. She's lying pressed against the chain link, as close as she can get to my normal sitting spot. My thought that she was desiccating was spot on, because she looks almost like the mummies I used to see on TV programs about ancient Egypt. Her skeleton is plainly visible, withered skin covering, but not hiding, the bones beneath. It looks like parts of her skin have broken down and rotted away, but for the most part, she is whole.

And wholly horrible.

She has no eyes, only black pits where they should be. Her nose is just a stubby remnant of its once perfect straightness. My mother was beautiful once. The only part of her that is still recognizable is her black hair and even that is dull and dirty. Great dust bunnies of it litter the floor where her shriveled scalp has lost its hold on those once-lustrous locks.

Her hand moves on the floor like a movie prop. It's stiff and gnarly, all bones, but it moves. Her jaw flexes a little as well. Even after a year, she is still animated to an extent. I don't need another year of wondering and keeping charts. I can tell by looking at her that it will be a very long time before the world is rid of the deaders. She's had no food, nothing, yet she still moves.

"Mom," I say.

The fingers twitch a little, but that's all. She can't come after me. If she could, she would have already.

I pick my sledgehammer up from the floor and walk over to her locked cage.

"Mom, I'll love you forever."

Today - As Good As It Gets

"Yeah, this place looks safe." I can't tell if she's being sarcastic or not. I don't know her well enough and the way she says it, I could take it either way. But, what I *can* say is that it's definitely not safe. Nowhere is truly safe. A place might be safe for an hour or a night, but safety is not a permanent state.

This particular building looks raggedy, almost like a horror movie set. Office chairs have been flung all over the messy strip of grass between the building and the small parking lot. The windows appear to have been busted out a long time ago, and for some reason there's a big flap of rotting carpet hanging out of an upstairs window.

Veronica snuggles the sleeping toddler closer to her chest and eyes me, apparently waiting for me to agree with her. I can see she's bone-tired. I might be carrying a pack and the weapons, but she's carrying a small human and another pack. Her human burden is also one that needs to be soothed when he gets upset so that he stays quiet. One that needs more

217

medical attention than my little first aid kit in the car could provide.

"It'll have to do. Stay here," I say and walk away. I know I should be more sympathetic, more friendly or something, but I just can't bear it. As soon as I smile, she'll get snatched and eaten or something. That's just been the whole tenor of this day. Shitty.

It's dirty inside, a little dark once I get away from the windows, and there isn't a single intact pane of glass, but there are a few windowless rooms and enough debris to pile against the doorways. It might do after all.

I wave them in and it takes a good while of futzing about to get Jon settled after being held all day. The butterfly bandages seem to be keeping the cut on his head closed, but he'll have a heck of a scar. It's strange, but even now, he's quiet and minds well. Sadly, I doubt kids who couldn't adjust to our new world survived for long. For Jon, I fear it will be all he'll ever know.

But maybe not.

The deaders will keep slowing, and maybe by the time he's old enough to understand just how much he missed out on, he might have a chance of getting it back. I hope so. Someone has to survive this world. Why not an adorable little kid with eyes as big as saucers and dimples in his cheeks?

While Veronica feeds Jon from the little stash I brought with me—my just-in-case satchel—I keep watch. A deader lumbers past, his mouth sucking on something that is painting his face bright red, but no in-betweeners. Just like everywhere else, there are birds all over the place here. Roosting in open windows and along roofs, their presence allows me to relax a little, grip my weapon just a little less tightly. They sent up an alarm when the deader went by. They'll do it again if more come.

Night falls and I keep the watch. The temptation to quiz her, to simply talk to another human, went away as soon as I saw how tired she was. Yawning almost as soon as the light faded, she seemed to be fighting the urge to lie down next to the sleeping boy. I convinced her it was okay. It's a good sign that they already trust me enough to sleep near me. And I confess, it feels very good to know there is another human nearby. I've missed humans so very much.

Of course, I have my practical reasons for wanting them rested in the morning. We've still got a long way to go and they haven't been eating much lately. Both of them are far too thin. They need to sleep to let the food they ate work on their bodies. I can't carry them home. They have to make it on their own two feet.

Veronica says she's fifteen. Fifteen seems so young to me now, but I wasn't much older than her when the world ended, and I was far less prepared and capable. Veronica is going to be busy with Jon, but I think she's going to be okay. At least, I think she will if I can just get her to my place.

There are perhaps four miles left to go, then we'll be there. We'll be home. Then I can show her how everything works, how to take care of the deaders at the fence, what to do if actual people show up. I can show her where all the emergency supplies are stashed and the best places to hide until she can escape in the off-chance that humans overrun the complex.

When I'm sure she's fully asleep and deep into dreamland—her breaths changing from the heavy ones of new sleep to the lighter breaths of true sleep—I roll up my pant leg. Under the light of the moon I can see the crescent-shaped wound that marks my calf. It's deep. Anything carried in that in-betweener's saliva is now inside my body, circulating in my blood.

This is my first bite. My mother got bitten and she turned in-betweener. Now I've been bitten too and for me, it's not just a matter of "if something happens."

Time, how much time?

Not much, I think. The headaches are back and now that there are other people to worry about, I can't pretend they aren't serious. I know what it means. Today is the first day I haven't had a headache in weeks, but that doesn't change the fact that I'm getting them. The same headaches as before. The same foggy pounding behind my ear.

This time, there are no medulloblastoma-eating nanites handy. It's only a matter of time until I take my mother's place in the cage. In a way, I suppose that's okay too. I'll have company to talk to me even after I'm gone. I like that idea. No matter what, I'll never be alone again.

And who knows what might happen before the worst comes to pass. I still have my mother's hard drive. I might make it to the military base. They might even have nanites there for the taking. It could happen. I won't give up hope. It's not in me to give up hope like that.

I look down at the two rings on my fingers. The gold shines almost coldly in the moonlight, but the stones twinkle with warmth. My mom's infinity ring and my own, side by side. I understand so much more now. There are so many things I wish I could tell her, but somehow I have this feeling she already knows.

Whatever the future holds is for us to discover as it unfolds before us. For now—for right now, this moment—I've got two people who are depending on me. I couldn't be happier about it. We'll figure out what comes next together. My heart lifts at that thought. *Together*. Who knew such a simple word could be so beautiful?

Happiness. Yeah, that's it exactly. I'm happy. You know what I mean?

Dear Reader

Thank you for reading!

I sure hope you liked what I did with my zombie apocalypse. The entire Between Life and Death trilogy is now complete. I originally intended this to be a stand-alone novel, a shorter book with an ambiguous ending that would capture the feeling of the end...long after it was over. I wanted to explore what it would be like for those who are left after most of the biting and entrail-showing is done?

The reception was awesome (thank you, readers!) so I created a trilogy in which all questions were answered, all loose ends neatly tied. You can continue the story (and get to know Veronica...who is an amazing character...in *Forever Between*.

Because Sam received so much email from readers who wanted to know his story, I've also written The Book of Sam. You can relive the apocalypse from day one with Sam, following along as he creates a family from those who have been left behind. Over 400 pages of tears and cheers…and Sam.

If you're the reviewing sort, please take a moment and leave a review on the site where you purchased this or on Goodreads (or both!). For the independent author, reviews absolutely make or break us. It takes only a few words and I would appreciate it enormously.

If you liked what you read, you can always sign up for my VIP Readers list and get some of my stories for free. You can do that here: http://eepurl.com/buDy4r

Rest assured, I never spam and always respect your privacy.

You can also find me all over social media, so let's connect!

About the Author

Ann Christy is a recently retired naval officer and secret writer. She lives by the sea under the benevolent rule of her canine overlords and a delusional cat. She's been known to call writing fiction a form of mental zombie-ism in reverse. She gets to put a little piece of her brain into yours and stay there with you—safely tucked away inside your gray matter—for as long as you remember her story. She hopes you enjoyed the meal.

Made in the USA
Middletown, DE
12 December 2021